BOUND BY LOVE

JANEAL FALOR

BOUND BY LOVE
Janeal Falor

ISBN-10:0-9897432-9-2
ISBN-13: 978-0-9897432-9-7

To learn more about this author, please visit: www.janealfalor.com

Cover Photo by Damonza
www.damonza.com

Print Interior by Write Dream Repeat Book Design LLC
www.wdrbookdesign.com

First Edition
10 9 8 7 6 5 4 3 2 1

For Karen
Thank you for being the best sister a girl could ask for

Chapter
ONE

T HE WIND PICKS up as I glance over the side of the boat. We're going fast, and the waves crash against us. Not much longer now before we're home. A day maybe, though there's still no land visible.

"Do you enjoy the open seas?" Robert asks, coming up next to me.

"They're nice enough, though I prefer land beneath my feet. At least this time, there have been no pirates, unlike the last couple of times I traveled by boat."

"Don't jinx us." But he says it with a laugh. "We're almost to Amara now. We should be good."

"Even with those in our way?" I point to the water and the large rocks ahead. We're steering straight for them.

"No. We should be turning already to get away from them."

We look up at the helm. No one's there.

Robert races toward it, and I hurry after him. When we get there, the wheel is tied in position. Robert curses, already fumbling to undo the knots. The wind picks up harder, the rocks growing closer.

"You're not going to get it untied in time," I yell.

Others become aware of the rocks. Jocelyn is out on the deck, looking at the rocks, sailors around her.

I pull out my sword. "Watch out."

One quick glance at me, and Robert is out of my way. I bring the sword down as hard as I can. Some of the threads break, but not all. I try to saw through the rope as we loom ever nearer. My hands shake. The boat is almost there. The rope snaps.

Robert turns the wheel, and the boat careens to the side, but not fast enough.

"Brace for impact," Robert hollers.

Everyone tries to find something to grab onto. Robert pulls me in his arms, and we hold on tight to each other.

The world veers as we smash into the rocks. Robert's yelling orders—something about a pump. The boat is steadier now, but from the way he's scowling and shouting, we're not in the clear yet. What if we sink? After everything I've survived, I can't imagine my life ending now.

"What can I do?" Not enough, I fear.

"Tell this wind to stop, so we can get steady again without fighting it."

That's something I can do. I take a few steps away from the chaos and let my power roam through me as I lift my arms in the air, palms out. The power flows out of me into the wind. I find the wind tugging against the sails, trying to pull us along, which would normally be good, but now makes finding our bearings harder.

I let my magic calm the wind. It struggles against my urgings, but it's life or death. I have to win. It can't overtake me. I pool my power together and shove it harder against the wind, effectively blocking it.

Robert pauses long enough to turn my way and say, "I didn't realize you'd be able to do that. Well done. Now we've just got to pump water out of the boat."

His words warm me, even if there are going to be consequences later. Hopefully when we're past this part of the ocean. A flurry of winds will probably blow, maybe even a storm, depending on how bad the consequences are. We should be home by then. If we can sail.

I twist my hand in my dress as I watch Robert. It's good to see him in his element. He's calm and reassuring, even as the others are panicking.

Jocelyn comes and stands beside me. "Do you know what's going on?"

"Only that they're trying to pump water out of the boat."

"That doesn't sound good," she says.

I shake my head. "No, but they haven't moved us to the lifeboats yet. I consider that a good sign."

She and I hover around the helm, trying to stay out Robert's way and not disrupt the others. Most of the work is done down below, where I can't see it.

After about an hour, the commotion slows, and Robert isn't talking with anyone. I go to his side. "Is everything going to be all right?"

He runs a hand through his hair, a crease forming above his eyebrows. "I think we'll make it to port. Right now, I'm more concerned with where the captain is and how he allowed this to happen. No one's seen him since this started."

Relief fills me. Since another sailor has taken up the wheel, I say, "Maybe we should check his cabin."

"You want to come with?"

"I do."

"All right, then. Let's go."

I give a quick word to Jocelyn, and Robert and I head for the Captain's quarters. Once we're there, Robert pulls out his sword.

"You think there's going to be trouble?" I whisper.

"I don't know, but I want to be prepared, just in case."

I pull out my own blade. No sense in not being ready.

Robert knocks on the door. There's no answer. He motions for me to go against the wall and then opens the door and checks the room.

I follow in after him, and I'm surprised at the sight. The captain, a balding human with a rounded belly, is sitting on his bed with a flask in his hand.

He glances at us, eyes bleary. "I was ready to go down with my ship," he says.

"You did this?" I ask.

He takes a swig out of his flask. "I hoped it would work. That I could prevent humans and elves from being together."

He doesn't seem like much of a threat, as drunk as he is, but I don't put away my sword.

"Is Captain Smythe behind this?" Robert asks in a stern voice.

"No. Only my own hopes of keeping you apart, even if it meant drowning with you." He sounds so dejected, I almost feel sorry for him. Then I remember he almost caused us to crash.

"You realize this is treason?" Robert asks.

The captain's only answer is to take another swig.

"Come on," Robert says. "We're taking you to the brig."

I follow them down to the brig, where Robert locks the captain in and sets a sailor to watch him. As we walk away, I say, "Are you all right? This is a lot to deal with."

"I don't know. I'm not sure I'm fit to be anything more than a sailor. Dealing with people is a lot harder than dealing with the sea."

I want to wrap my arms around him, to comfort him, but it's still awkward after being engaged to his best friend. Instead, I say, "You handled that perfectly. I think there's more strength in you than you know."

"Maybe. I guess we will find out," he says. "We should have brought Captain Zaccheus with us."

"You know he's loyal?"

"I trust him with my life, unlike everyone else we've run into. Unfortunately, he's off on a trade route."

I wish I knew how to fix this, but I have no words. I have nothing helpful. All I have are my own fears.

"I hope this isn't a sign of what we have to face when we're married," he says. "Is everyone going to oppose us?"

They may very well try to.

Chapter
TWO
⁀

I SEE MY CITY in the distance across the water, green
and beautiful. My almost-forgotten bedroom waits for
me in the white castle up on the hill. Somehow it doesn't
seem as much like home as it used to. I've been through too
much for Princess Arabella's elaborate bedroom to feel like
mine. For living in a castle to feel like me. And yet, as much
as I've tried to be someone else, there's no denying Princess
Arabella is who I am.

Robert takes my hand, and a peaceful feeling settles over
me. *Prince Robert.* It's hard to remember he's Abner's cousin
and was third in line for the throne. After Abner's demise, the
human king delegated him to be next in line to rule Bardus.
And right now, captain of the ship.

It's difficult to think that Abner is really gone. That he died
defending me. I didn't like him all that much to begin with,
but he was growing on me. I had forgiven him for making me

believe Robert was dead, and I was prepared to marry him. To know he died saving me makes me feel no small amount of guilt. His last words being a declaration of his love for my best friend, Jocelyn, makes the guilt even greater. If only he was still alive and the two of them could get married to further unite our people.

At least Octavian, my parent's old advisor, and Aiden, an elf with the power to stop spells, are both headed for my parents, to be sentenced for a conspiracy against both humans and elves. In fact, they should be here. Part of me hopes their sentences have already been carried out; I don't have the stomach for watching an execution. Another part of me thinks I need to be there. I need to say what they have done and make sure neither of them can ever get free to repeat their actions.

Robert removes his hand from mine and puts his arm around my shoulder as the boat gently rocks. "Thinking heavy thoughts again?"

I'm still having a hard time believing he's next to me, reading me so well. I only wish I could do the same, but thoughts of being engaged to Abner make it hard. Not that I care for him like I do Robert, but it's still hard knowing I was going to marry Robert's best friend. "It's difficult not to, considering the circumstances."

He gives me a squeeze and presses a kiss to my forehead. I want to lean into him, to savor his closeness, but something stops me. Something that I think has to do with Abner.

"I suppose it's hard not to dwell on the heavy, the way things have gone," he says, "but I hate to see you down."

I smile. "It's hard to stay down with you around. I only hope there are no more obstacles with our wedding."

He grins, glancing at my lips. "As long as we're together in the end."

Which I still can't believe. I never thought I'd be able to marry the man I love, and here I am, taking him home to my parents before our big wedding day.

Only Abner and Constance's deaths hang heavy in my cheery thoughts. I wish they were both here—but that Abner was here not as the prince. Constance was murdered by Captain Smythe right before my eyes, and it still haunts me. My nightmares feel like they'll never end.

"Look at you two," Jocelyn says, coming up beside us on the deck. "You're too adorable together."

Though her words are upbeat and her lips are smiling, there's a deeper sadness lingering in her gaze. One brought on by Abner's death. I don't know how to help, other than by being her friend.

It's a reminder that, no matter how happy I feel, everything isn't perfect.

THE STREETS ARE FILLED with elves staring at me and Robert as we pass by in the carriage. It makes me want to cringe away. To hide on the floor. Memories flood in, of the last time I was in a carriage with a human man. With Abner. An arrow was shot at me, and he gave his life in exchange for mine. I can't handle that happening again.

This time is different, though. We're in Amara. There are no elf haters here because we're mostly elves. Not all of us, though. There are some human guards as well as elf guards with us. And that doesn't mean my people can't attack Robert.

What if they do? The way they're eyeing him is clearly without trust. With nothing but fear and suspicion.

I lean closer to him, hoping it shows we're really together, not merely sharing a carriage. Of course, there's no guarantee we'll marry. My parents have to approve of him first. I can't imagine them not approving since he now has the position Abner did. He will be a leader to the humans someday. There's no reason for my parents not to accept him, but still I fear.

"You're doing it again," Robert says.

"Doing what?"

"Worrying."

"I know." I sigh. "It's hard not to. So much has gone wrong, I can't imagine things going right for a change."

"But they will." He grabs my hand and gives it a squeeze. Peace settles through me. He's right. We have a chance. If only I could get my worries to understand that.

We near the castle. Everything I've missed, and yet, I'm not sure how I feel about coming back. Everything is so different now. I'm different. I don't know how I'll fit in any more. Ever since my face changed to look more like a human's because of the spell I cast to mask my appearance, things have been more strained. Courtiers give me long glances. Elves don't talk to me. Things are tough. They may get even tougher.

Still, no one's yelling or throwing things at us. Maybe they're as nervous as I am about what's coming.

"Do you think they can come to accept us?" I ask Robert.

"I know they can. You're a good person. They already welcome you. With time, they'll come to receive me too."

"You hope."

He runs a hand through his hair. "It's true. I don't know for certain. I hope they accept me. I believe they will."

I want to rest my head on his shoulder, but with so many onlookers, I need to maintain suitable decorum. "Me too."

We pull through the gates of the castle. I breathe a sigh of relief. I'm grateful to be out of the crowd's eye. Of course, soon I'll be in my parents', and I'm not certain that's any better. Last time I saw them, I was getting married to Abner. They were sitting there— my father looking expectant, Mother reminding me to be proper. That's how I always think of them. How I know they are. Will they be the same after everything that's happened?

Will Mother still have a hard time looking at me? Since my looks changed, she can't seem to even glance at me. It would be nice if she did, but I fear her reaction if she did. She called me ugly. She doesn't mean to hurt my feelings; she's just not used to my new face. Sheesh—I'm not used to it either. Whatever am I supposed to do about looking like a human elf instead of the girl I saw in the mirror growing up?

Keep plugging along and hope things get better.

We pull up to the main entrance, and the carriage stops.

"Are you ready for this?" Robert asks.

"As ready as I'll ever be."

Which is to say, not at all.

Chapter
THREE
∾

GUARDS STAND on both sides of the door to the throne room. My hand shakes as one of them reaches for the handle. How will my parents react to seeing me? Will they still look over me, unable to face me since I look less like an elf and more like a human? Will they reject my new fiancé, despite him being a prince?

The door opens, and I'm ushered inside, Robert at my side. I hold my head high, like Mother taught me. The throne room seems bigger than I remember. My parents are off in the distance. I have to get closer before I can make out what they're doing. Mother's gaze is on her hands, but Father jumps out of his chair and rushes straight for me. I've never seen him move so fast in my life.

As soon as he reaches me, he envelops me in a hug, warm and comforting. His arms are tight around me, and I find my eyes tearing up. I've never received such an embrace from my father before, and this is making me wish it were a common practice. I've missed him so much. I can't imagine what he must have gone through since I was kidnapped.

When we pull apart, I'm surprised to find tears in his eyes as well.

"I thought I lost you," he says. "After Captain Smythe stole you away, I didn't think we'd ever see you again. I thought you were gone for a second time. I couldn't bear it."

He pulls me back in for a second hug.

"It's all right," I say. "I'm fine now. I'm safe. I made it here." Even with losing the captain of our ship. Thank goodness Robert knew what to do in that situation. My father pulls away but takes hold of my hand. My daddy. "It's good to be home."

"It's good to have you here." He looks next to me. "And who's this you brought with you? A sailor?"

I turn toward Robert, heat creeping up my neck. "This is Prince Robert. He's now next in line for the throne of Bardus. With your permission, he's my fiancé."

"Your fiancé?" He gives Robert a once over. "Why don't you both come over to the thrones, and we'll discuss it with the queen?"

Not the direct approval I was looking for, but not a rejection either. There's hope. If they find Robert half as charming as I do, they'll be more than happy to make him their son-in-law.

But what if they don't? Last time mother saw him as a common sailor, and she rejected him. But then he was a simple human, not someone who could help assure peace between our countries. And, he's not Abner.

I push the doubts away and follow Father to the thrones. Instead of sitting on his, he stays next to me. It's nice that he's showing more love than he has the rest of my life combined. I try to make eye contact with Mother, but she stares straight ahead, as if I'm not there.

I want to twist my hand in my dress, but I know she abhors the habit. I don't need to give her another reason to be upset with me.

"This is Prince Robert," my father tells my mother before turning to Robert. "We're both so sorry for the loss of your Prince Phillip. Our condolences."

"Thank you. We bear it with a heavy heart," Robert says.

I ache to think of it.

My father turns back to mother. "Because of Prince Phillip's demise, Prince Robert has asked for our daughter's hand in marriage."

"And you've given your approval?" Mother asks, voice smooth and calm.

"Not yet. I thought we could all talk it over together."

Mother gazes at Robert, though she still avoids looking at me despite the fact that I'm right next to him. "And what other credentials do you hold, besides being a prince, that make you worthy of my daughter's hand?"

The question gives me hope that she still cares about me, even if she can't bring herself to glance at me. I hope she doesn't give Robert too hard a time.

"I love her and will cherish her as long as I live," Robert says.

My heart flutters at his words, but it's stilted, stuck remembering I was engaged to his best friend.

"That sounds very endearing," Mother says. "Tell me about your family."

I'd feel more comfortable if she wasn't questioning him. That she'd accept him more readily like my father has, but I suppose that if she doesn't know things about him like I do, it's natural to want to protect your daughter. Though I bet Father has researched him thoroughly since getting the message about what took place with Robert becoming the new heir.

"My mother is a wealthy business owner and ruler over Derelinquo Fork. My father helps with both the businesses and the city. They are hoping to make better trade with our two countries. My mother is King Mark's sister. My family has served Bardus faithfully for generations."

"Trade, you say?" My father rubs his chin. "We're all very interested in increasing trade."

"Yes," Mother says. "Better trade routes would be most welcome."

"It's settled, then. A wedding we shall have," Father says. "After we've had a proper mourning time for Prince Philip."

"There's one other thing." I can't believe I'm about to add more time before finally getting married to Robert, but I can't imagine going through with the wedding without having properly taken care of Constance. "I'm in mourning for Constance. Have you held a funeral for her?"

Father gives Mother a look I don't understand, and then says, "There's been no funeral yet, but we can have one now. She's officially been buried, but we can have a ceremony just the same. And then the wedding?"

I cringe. "I want to get married—I really do—but I don't feel good about it being directly after Constance's funeral. There's some information I'd like to search for, at Pomum Heart. Information about some lost scrolls that have to do with our history. Maybe after the funeral we can seek it out and have the wedding afterward. It would give us the proper time to mourn Prince Philip."

"I don't know… I hate to think of you going about the country after everything that's happened."

"I'd keep her safe, sir," Robert says. "And we could take some guards. Arabella is onto some information she found from some scrolls, concerning the history of both our people. I think looking into it more would be a wise use of our time."

"And you don't mind postponing the wedding?" Father asks.

"Not for this reason. No," he replies. "Besides, I know about arranged marriages, but it would be a good chance for Arabella and me to get to know one another better."

I love the idea. Of course I know him, but not as an engaged couple. There are still things we need to speak of. Before I can say anything, Mother speaks up. "I think it's a sound plan, though I do believe I should go with you, to chaperone. It's been a while since I went around to the people anyhow, and it's best I spend some time with my daughter."

Hope flares within me. "You really want to go with us?"

"I do not just consider it my duty, but my desire," she replies, making my hope flame brighter, though she's still avoiding looking at my face.

"It's not the easiest of journeys," I say. "We could take a carriage, of course, but I don't know how long the search will take or where it will lead us."

"All the more reason for me to go. Besides, I've traveled all over this country. More than you have. Been doing so since before I became queen. I think I can manage a little trip."

"Thank you," I say. "I can't wait to spend some time with you."

She sniffs, a dainty little sound. "Yes, well, I only want what's best for my daughter."

If she wasn't so opposed to public displays of affection, I would run up right now and give her a hug.

"It's settled, then," my father says. "We'll have a ceremony to remember Constance, followed by your journey to look for the lost scrolls—with several guards, I might add—and finally, we will have your wedding. We delay too long. There have already been too many problems."

"*That* we can agree on," I say. "The last thing I want to do is wait longer than necessary."

"Soon, our two nations shall be united," my father says.

And I will be married to the man I love.

Chapter
FOUR
⌢

BEFORE WE CAN HOLD Constance's ceremony, there's something we need to take care of—Octavian and Aiden. They've been in the dungeons since their arrival a few days ago. It's time to punish them. Octavian's is guaranteed. He was banished, and he left the island he was exiled to. That's a death sentence, for sure. Aiden I'm not so certain on. Whatever happens to them, I don't want to be around for it.

We sit in the throne room. I'm near my parents, the courtiers interested in attending on both sides of the room. I guess I'm the only one who doesn't want to see a man sentenced to death.

Robert is nearby, though Jocelyn decided against attending. I want to be with her, but here I am, doing my duty.

The doors open, and Aiden is brought in first. He doesn't look nearly as cocky as the last time I saw him. His head is hanging down, his hands in chains before him. He has a guard on each side, though they don't touch him.

When Aidan reaches the thrones, my father stands. "You are brought before us today, charged with crimes against the state. Most specifically, crimes against my daughter and heir to the throne. What have you to say?"

Aiden looks up, but his gaze remains unfocused. "I have nothing to say."

My father stares at him, silent. He's probably thinking of a suitable punishment. Some of me hopes it's nothing to do with death, but the rest of me remembers what happened when Octavian was allowed to live. It's not an easy decision.

My father says, "You have not made this easy for me. You've not committed a crime before, so I will not have you executed, but conspiring and assisting in the kidnapping of my daughter is treason. You are hereby sentenced to the dungeons for twenty years, at which time I will speak to you again concerning your future."

Aiden's shoulders slump.

While the sentence is fair, I feel sorry for him. I remember him in Captain Smythe's cave, while the humans tortured Jocelyn and called her an elf lover. The look on his face... I have to think he's not all bad. But then, maybe most people who do wrong aren't all bad. Maybe there's always at least a little good in people.

Aiden turns, and the guards lead him out. As soon as he's gone, two new guards lead in Octavian, each holding him by an arm. Octavian holds his head high, a smirk across his face. I don't know what he expects, but he doesn't look ready to be sentenced.

When the three of them get to the thrones and stop, my heart beats recklessly. I can't handle whatever's to come. It's going to be harsh, whatever it is. The look on Octavian's face makes my skin crawl. I force myself to sit still, though I want to squirm. I exchange a glance with Robert. He appears to be just as uncomfortable as I am.

"What are you going to do to me?" Octavian asks with a laugh. "Banish me again? Good luck with that. Wherever I go, I will always return."

My father doesn't hesitate. "Tie his mouth shut. I don't want to hear a single thing out of it."

One of the guards does so, but Octavian continues smirking throughout the process.

My father says, "I was lenient before. Too lenient, it would seem." His jaw is rigid. This is harder for him than he's making it appear. Octavian was Father and Mother's advisor for years before this happened. Sometimes I forget that. "You are hereby sentenced to death by hanging," Father says, "to take place immediately in the palace courtyard. I want all women and children to remain inside while it takes place."

Octavian fights the guards, pulling against them with all his might. I stiffen in my chair, wondering what will happen should he get free. The guards are too strong for him, though. Not only does he not get free, but he's dragged outside.

Robert moves by my side. "Are you all right?"

I feel a little faint, but otherwise— "I will be, once this is all over. I'm grateful my father said women will stay here. I don't want to watch."

"I'm glad as well. It's not something I want to watch either, but I need to do my duty, to make certain he will never harm you again." He gives my hand a squeeze.

It's hard not to be scared, but I put on a brave face for him. "I will see you soon."

"Not soon enough." He winks at me, and then he's gone with the crowd.

The women are gathering in groups throughout the room, gossiping about what happened, no doubt. There hasn't been a death sentence here as long as I can remember.

None of the women approach me. Whether it's because of my looks or because they're shy of approaching me on the throne, I may never know. If Jocelyn was here, she'd be sure to come over. It's just as well. This has left me with a lot to consider. I'm going to have to make these type of tough decisions when I'm ruler of this country. I hope that it's not for a while and that my father lives a long, long time.

Chapter
FIVE

⌒

C ONSTANCE'S CEREMONY is short and to the
point like she would have wanted it. Those gathered
remember her, but I feel that none of them knew her
quite as I did. Though she didn't tell me everything, she was
like a mother to me.

Most of the royal court shows up, surprising me. Not many
of them know me well, but I suppose anything their princess
does, they feel they need to do. I don't think Constance would
have cared one way or the other.

Robert stays with me throughout the ceremony. Though
we don't hold hands, his presence is comforting enough.
Jocelyn is also nearby. Constance was as much of a mother
to her as she was to me. I move closer and put an arm around
her. Her cheeks are wet.

I don't cry. Not here, and not with everyone watching. Not
when they need me to be strong. I've cried and cried over her;
this feels more like a goodbye than mourning. A goodbye for

a person I loved dearly and still love, though she's no longer with us.

"It is time for us to remember her," the officiator says. "To remember her life. I have here a note, written about her.

"Constance was kind and loving but hid it behind a tough exterior. She showed everyone what to do and took the time for the smallest task to the largest. She loved fiercely and deeply, even from years apart. No other could get to someone's heart like she. Her food was excellent and made with feeling like no one else. She touched the hearts of many, saving children when everyone else looked the other way. Her heart was the softest, gentlest one we could ever know, despite how she tried to show us otherwise."

The officiator stops and puts the note in his pocket. "No truer words were ever spoken. She was the most excellent of women. I suggest we all take a few minutes to remember her in our hearts."

I do as he says, thinking about her while Jocelyn wipes away her tears. I can't imagine life without Constance, though it's been a while since she passed. I keep expecting her to pop up around every corner. To tell me what to do or not to do. More, to give me that look that says she isn't going to give me her opinion but knows what I should chose.

Life will never be the same without her.

I'm not the only one who thinks so. A ways off from us stands Andries. Though not a tear falls down his cheek, his expression is of one in the deepest of mourning. I can't imagine what it must be like to love someone so much for years and years, but never be able to marry them. To never be able to spend time with them, loving and cherishing them. There must be so much weight pressing down on him.

And to think, if I was never born, Constance would have spent her life with him. She would never have been put in Captain Smythe's path, and so she'd still be among the living. I know she wouldn't want me to think this way. She'd want me to continue with my life with as little disruption as possible.

But no matter how I go on, I'll always remember her.

The ceremony ends. People drop flowers on her grave. It's soon littered with them, and though it is pretty, I don't do it myself. She understood how I feel about cutting plants down; she would understand. Maybe when I come back from Pomum Heart, I will plant something special near her grave. A flower bush or a tree. Something simple but a good reminder of her.

Andries is the last to drop a flower. He gives me a simple nod and moves on. Jocelyn goes with him, a little piece herself of what Constance worked to make better. Jocelyn wouldn't be here with me if it wasn't for Constance. If Constance has to be gone, at least I still have time with my best friend.

As I head away from the gathering, Robert is at my side. He asks, "How are you feeling?"

"Sad. Torn. I don't know. I wish she was still here." I want to take his hand, but something stops me. I shouldn't let it. We're to be married after all, but it stops me anyway.

"She was a good woman."

"The best." Tears well up in my eyes.

Reginald comes up to me. Not exactly what I want at this moment, but I blink away the tears and give a gracious smile.

As my parents' advisor since Octavian's removal, he has a lot of power. He was Octavian's assistant before all this.

"I hear you're going on a journey." His nasal tone grates on me. I suppose it's not his fault his voice sounds like that, but does he have to intrude now?

"You heard correctly."

Robert moves closer to me, supporting me.

Reginald says, "I'm to go with you."

I try not to cringe, instead walking a little faster. "When was this decided?"

"Last night. The king and I talked." He speaks as if he knows my father better than I do. "He agrees my expertise on humans would be perfect for this journey. He can get along with his other advisors while I'm giving you the guidance you need."

Perfect? Just what we need. Someone who is conceited when it comes to everything human. Not like we have an actual human going with us already. This trip is getting more crowded by the minute. I hope we don't find anything so sensitive I wouldn't want prying eyes to see.

Chapter
SIX

༉

AFTER WORKING ON THEM all morning, the last of the carriages is loaded. It's time to go. I find myself wishing I could go on horseback instead of in the carriage, but I'll be with Robert and Mother. It would be nice if Reginald wouldn't be there too. Oh, well... Perhaps I'll discover he's not as annoying a person as I've found him to be until now. Or he could be worse.

I want to see Jocelyn off in her carriage—maybe even sneak in with her—but with Mother here, there's no getting around proper etiquette. I'll have to give in and do what I should. For now.

Many guards are coming along with us, both human and elf. I hope they won't be needed.

I let Robert help me up into the carriage, my fingers tingling where they meet his. Mother is already in and situated, so I don't let my hand linger as much as I'd like. I move to take the bench across from her, but she pats the seat next to her. "Come sit by me."

Interesting. Perhaps it's so it's easier not to look at me. Then again, maybe I'm being too hard on her. She could just want to be near me.

I settle in next to her. This is the closest I remember being to her. When we've been on trips, she always sits next to my father. This is different. Good or bad, I'm not sure. Probably somewhere in between.

Reginald gets in next, followed by Robert, who sits across from me. I wish we were next to each other so I could hold his hand. Give that tiny brush of skin. It doesn't matter, though. My thoughts drift to Abner, his best friend. What does he think of marrying his best friend's fiancée? Now isn't the time to ask.

Andries insisted on riding on horseback. If he gets tired, Robert or Reginald can switch with him, or he can join Jocelyn and mother's servants. I may even get a chance to ride. Probably not, but a girl can hope.

The horses pull on, and we're off. I wonder what it is we're going to find in Pomum Heart. Hopefully it's easy enough to find the scrolls, though if it was too easy, they'd have been found by now—which is a possibility. What if they're gone? What if we never find them? It's a history of our people I'm most anxious to have.

No sense worrying about it until we know for certain.

We ride for hours and hours. Sometimes we talk, but often I look out the window or try to rest. With Reginald here, it's hard to strike a conversation with my mother. Or even for that matter, have a personal conversation with Robert. I hoped traveling with him would give us time to become accustomed to each other as an engaged couple, but with others here, it's hard to talk about much. Everything feels too personal. Perhaps I'm making too big a deal of it.

"Can you tell us a little bit about your life growing up, Robert?" I ask, hoping I'm not putting him on the spot.

"Yes, do tell us," Mother says.

He sits up straighter. I suppose it's not every day you're questioned by your future mother-in-law, especially one who is a queen.

"Well, I was born and raised in Omanska. I grew up third in line for the throne, so I always knew someday it was possible for me to inherit it, though I honestly hoped it would never happen."

I want to give his hand a squeeze. Instead, I gently tap my foot against his.

He continues. "I spent some time in the military."

"Really?" my mother says. "What did you do there?"

Reginald gives him a calculating look that makes me wonder what he's thinking.

"Mostly, I trained. There's never been a time of war, so our biggest fight is with pirates."

"You fought pirates as a soldier?" I want to be worried about it, but he's still here and safe, which confirms he made it out fine.

"A little. Never anyone as ruthless as Captain Smythe. My captain tried to keep me out of the action, but it was still a good learning experience."

I remember him fighting pirates, almost dying in my arms. I thought he did die. It's troubling. "I'm just glad you're safe."

"Me too."

"Is that where you learned to fight with a sword so well?" I ask.

"It is where I got better at the skill. Abner—I mean Prince Phillip," he says, glancing at my mother, "and I had lessons growing up." His voice takes on a wistful tone. "Phillip never did enjoy lessons quite as much as I did. I could almost always best him because of it, but he somehow made it fun."

I reach across the carriage, not caring that Mother and Reginald are here watching. Some things a person just has to do. I take Robert's hand and give it a squeeze. "He was a good friend."

"Yes, he was."

I sit back into my seat, wishing I'd seen more of that side of Abner sooner, instead of only a little bit of who he was at the end. I wonder if he was more like Robert than what I knew of him. I suppose I'll never know more than what I hear from stories now. I got to know his kindness a little, before he gave his life for mine. With his last words, he wasn't just looking out for our kingdoms, but my and his best friend's happiness. It's not fair. Not at all.

Now I have the chance to get to know his best friend. Someone I want to make *my* best friend.

Robert.

I smile up at him, and he smiles back. There's no shying away from him. He gives me a look of utter adoration. I hope I never do anything to make that go away.

Chapter
SEVEN
∾

W E STOP AT AN INN for the night. There's not much here, other than the inn, so it makes me feel both safe and a little nervous—safe from elves being upset by Robert's presence and nervous that pirates or other enemies might catch up with us. We have plenty of guards, though, and I have my sword. We're well prepared for anything, but I hope nothing happens.

I make my way inside. The wooden floors gleam in the candlelight. There are round tables with chairs scattered throughout the room, but they're all empty. The innkeeper and his wife watch from behind a bar, gazes fixed on Robert and me. Jocelyn leads me up the stairs off to the right side and down a narrow hall with rugs softening the floor to the room we're sharing for the night.

I give my goodnights to mother and Robert.

"There's no one else staying at the inn tonight," Jocelyn says. "It's just us."

I sigh. "I suppose that's for the best."

"Would you rather there be people?"

"Yes and no. I'd like for more elves to have the opportunity to see me and Robert together, to get a chance to know him and what a wonderful person he is. But it's also nice not to have to worry about anyone but the inn keeper and his family giving me and Robert weird looks."

"I think the inn keeper was more in awe seeing you, than giving you a weird look."

"Yes, but his wife—"

"Must have something wrong with her eyes to stare at you like that," Jocelyn says. "That may be how she looks at royalty she's never seen before." When I don't say anything, she continues. "The change in your appearance is still bothering you, isn't it?"

I hesitate to give an honest answer, but this is Jocelyn. She knows me about as well as anyone else in the world does. "Yes. It's hard to look so different. I was used to people looking at me with awe, not confusion, and at times, even revulsion." Not that they have to look at me that way; I just don't know how to deal with these strange looks. I can't blame them, though. It's hard to glance at my own reflection, let alone having others see me all the time.

"I'm sorry. I wish I had some words of wisdom for you, but I don't. It shouldn't have to be this way. People shouldn't be staring at you like that—especially not other elves. They have no place to judge you. You are perfect the way you are."

My chest warms, but it doesn't change what I see in the mirror. "Thank you for that."

"Of course. Now tell me. How is it riding in the carriage with your beloved all day?"

I giggle. "It would be wonderful, except for the fact that Reginald and Mother are there."

"Oh, so you want alone time with him, do you?"

My face heats.

"I thought so. You're so in love."

"I am." I give a happy sigh. "It's quite the giddy feeling. I've never experienced anything like it before." I hesitate a moment, but then I force myself to bring it up. "What about you? How are you doing after Abner died?" We haven't talked about him since it happened. I don't know how she feels about it at all, other than sad.

"I'm not at my best, to be honest. I didn't know him as well as you know Robert, but yes, I was developing feelings for him." She gives me a glance that looks like she feels guilty for telling me that. It can't be easy talking to me, his almost wife, about her feelings for him. "He was nicer than I first thought him to be, and he grew kinder all the time. There was something about him that made my heart patter. I tried to resist those feelings knowing that he could never be mine, but they existed nonetheless."

"Did you know he loved you?"

She shakes her head, tears forming in her eyes. "No. He never said it before. We only had so many chances to talk without being overheard. Or probably because he either didn't know himself, or out of loyalty to you and your upcoming nuptials. That was why I didn't allow myself to feel more for him. I held back as much as I could. I knew you two were to be married, and no feelings I had would change that."

"It would be nice if things could have been different. He would have been a much better fit for you than he was for me. You deserved to be together."

"But it will never be." She cries, and I wrap my arms around her. Her tears continue as I comfort her the best I can. Funny thought I used to be unable to touch another person, and here I am, embracing her.

A few minutes later, she gains control of herself and pulls back, though her voice is still weepy. "Thank you. I wish things were different too. Why is love so hard?"

"I don't know."

"I guess we'll never know for sure." She lets out a puff of air. "Come on. It's time to get ready for bed. We've got a long trip ahead of us tomorrow."

"Oh, joy. More time with Reginald." He makes me shiver.

She hands me my nightgown and helps me with the ties in the back. "Did he say much today?"

"Thankfully, no. He was enraptured with Robert talking but didn't say much himself."

"Not interesting like us humans." She gives a little laugh.

"He was sitting right next to one. You'd think that'd be enough to keep him awake."

She laughs harder, and then sobers. "Really, I'm grateful I'm not in the same carriage as him. There's something about him that gives me the creeps."

"I know what you mean. I feel the same way."

"And you have to share the carriage with him the entire journey. It would make my day if you and Robert could come back and ride with me and your mother's servants could go with him."

"Me too. The problem is Mother would never go for it."

"It's just as well. You and Robert would probably rather have a carriage to yourselves."

My cheeks heat. I seem to be doing a lot of that lately. I didn't know being with Robert would have this consequence.

"We'd best get to bed for the night," I say, hurrying to change the subject.

She giggles. "I guess so. Someone needs to dream of their prince."

My cheeks heat more.

"That's what I thought," she says. "I'll talk to you in the morning."

As I go to bed, I think of her words about Robert—and yes, how nice it would be to spend some time alone with him. But it's not going to happen until after the wedding. It goes against propriety. I also think of what Jocelyn said about Abner. I wish there was something I could do to fix things.

Some things are impossible to fix.

Chapter
EIGHT
❧

THE REST OF THE JOURNEY is like before, though with less talking. We make several more stops along the way, getting those wary looks from people. At least I'm with Robert; that's what really matters. Once we reach our destination village, I'm even more anxious to find the scrolls.

Pomum Heart. It has more apple trees than I remember. They're everywhere. The air is sweet-scented.

I hope Emeline's reception is as sweet. As we pull into the inn, I grow jittery. I haven't seen Emeline since she was sent here to do service work with the children in the hopes that it would help her learn to be a better person. It's hard to imagine what her greeting will be like. If she'll be angry at me for being part of the reason she ended up working here, or—less likely—if she'll be grateful for a place to work instead of going to jail or being exiled. I wonder how I'll feel upon seeing her again.

The carriage stops, and Robert gets out first and then takes my hand to help me down. He gives me a squeeze, which reassures me. Whatever Emeline is like, I won't have to do this by myself.

Perhaps we'll be lucky and not run into her.

Mother gets out next, letting Robert help her from the carriage. She's stately, like always. I don't know how she manages to look so fresh and beautiful when we've been riding for five days. It's one thing she didn't pass down onto me.

Jocelyn meets us just outside. Between her and Robert, I have enough back up. Plus, the guards are close by in case something serious happens. But it won't. Everything will be fine.

"How was your ride today?" I ask Jocelyn, wishing I could have been with her.

"Boring." She leans in and whispers, "Your mother's lady does nothing but snore."

I hold in a snicker, but my mother seems to know it's about to come out of me, and she gives me the eye from her place, several steps away.

"With any luck, you'll be able to room with me." We've roomed together the entire trip, but that doesn't mean we'll share one here. It could be that they have another room off of mine where she'll stay.

"Luck is what I need right now."

The doors to the inn open, and we leave our conversation for now.

"Greetings, Your Majesties." An older woman with a mole on her chin bows to us. "Please follow me, and I'll get you settled."

Straight to our rooms. I couldn't have hoped for anything better. We follow her through the door and a corridor. The wood is dark and rich, like melted chocolate. There isn't really any décor, but it's not needed with how elegant the wood is.

We've gone a short ways when we run into another person. Emeline. Only she doesn't look like the Emeline I remember. Sure, she's still round with rosy cheeks and pouty lips, but something about her face has changed. A new light is in her eyes that wasn't there before.

She curtseys as we pass, and then stops us. "Just a moment, please."

"Yes?" Robert says.

I'm thankful. I don't know what to say to her. I don't know if I can talk yet.

"I heard you had arrived, and I just wanted to tell Princess Arabella—well, all of you—that I'm sorry for my behavior. I should have never trusted Octavian and his words. He was cunning, but still, I shouldn't have fallen for it."

That's the new look about her. Serenity. Can I forgive her after everything she put me through? The silence stretches as my thoughts tumble about. I want to forgive her, but it's a hard thing she's asking of me. If it wasn't for her, things could have turned out much differently. Constance and Abner might still be alive.

We've learned good information about Captain Smythe, though, and taken care of Octavian permanently. Emeline could have been as much of a victim as I was. "I accept your apology. Thank you for taking the time to do so."

She gives another curtsey and hurries down the hall. The rest of the way to our rooms is a blur. I can't concentrate on anything after hearing her apologize. It's the last thing I expected. What did she do that changed her so? Whatever it is, I'm grateful my father sent her here instead of to prison. It seems he made the correct choice.

When we get to our rooms, Jocelyn and I find we are to share a room if we want. There are two beds in my room and plenty of drawer space. I couldn't be happier with the arrangement. I haven't had enough time to talk to her lately. I thought having her come on the journey would help, but with being in different carriages, those hopes were dashed.

"Your things will be sent up shortly," the woman with the mole on her chin says.

"Thank you."

As soon as the door closes behind us, Jocelyn says, "I can't believe that just happened. I never thought I'd live to see Emeline apologize."

"Neither did I. I can't imagine what must have come over her," I say. "Best yet, we do get to share a room. I hope you don't mind not having one of your own."

"It's fine. And certainly better than having to share a room with Miss Snores-a-lot. I don't know how your mother can sleep in the same room as her."

"She does amazing things with Mother's hair. That must make up for it."

"Maybe I'll have to find out a few tricks from her."

I shrug. "Whatever you like. I know there are times I need to be fancier, but I'm just as happy to have my hair down, wild and free."

She giggles. I stop to look around, as does Jocelyn. There's dark wood throughout, but white fabric on the canopy bed, and the two large windows brighten up the room. The curtains are also white. There are two queen-sized beds and a vanity with a bowl and pitcher on it.

What I like most, though, are the paintings. They are rich jewels that show the landscape around Pomum Heart. Apples everywhere and trees thick with fruit. Though the people in the images are unfamiliar, their cheery faces help bring a light in.

"This is a lovely room," Jocelyn says.

"It is. I'm grateful we'll get to stay here for the duration of our visit in Pomum Heart." The reason we came here, though—will we be able to accomplish it, or will we be thwarted? It doesn't seem possible right now that we'll be successful. "Do you think we'll be able to find the scrolls?"

She drops what she was doing and comes over to me. "I don't know. In all likelihood, they could be destroyed or long gone, found by someone else who did who knows what with them. Not to get you down, but realistically, we haven't a clue where they could be, if they're even here. I'm not sure we'll find them. Not sure at all."

"I want you to be wrong, but I fear you're right." I sit on the bed. "I don't want to put off my wedding, looking forever for something that isn't there, but I do believe we'll find something that tells of our history."

"Do you think if you do, it will really help with what's going on now?"

"I can only hope." Because without help, there's more pressure on Robert and me to fix things ourselves. What I want is answers for my people. Answers I hope to find in our history.

Chapter
NINE

∾

ONCE WE'VE GOTTEN settled and made sure our things arrived safely, we wander out into the building. We make it through the hallway, back to the entrance, when we run into the lady who took care of us when we arrived.

She's bright and cheery. "We're so excited to have you join us, Princess Arabella. Your maid too," she says.

"This is Jocelyn, my lady in waiting," I reply.

The woman lifts an eyebrow but doesn't comment on my lack of servants. "I am Catarrha."

"It's lovely to meet you," I say. "Thank you for your warm welcome."

"The welcome isn't over. If you'll follow me, we have a celebration for you coming to visit our small town."

"That's so kind of you." But I'd rather get to work on finding where those scrolls could be hidden.

"Dinner is ready, and your guests are waiting. I hope you don't mind my taking you now. The queen said she won't be ready for a while yet."

"That's fine." Mother likes her entrances, anyway. "Where's Prince Robert?" It's strange to put Prince before his name, but I need to remember to use the title out of respect.

"He's already there, waiting for you."

That holds some comfort. That, and being with my people. I enjoy getting to interact with them. It's not something I get to do nearly often enough, especially lately.

We move through another hall and come out to a courtyard full of people. It's bustling and smells of sweetly scented apples. It's no wonder, for the tables are laden with food, much of which appears to be apples.

When we enter the courtyard, everyone stands and curtsies or bows. I wave as quickly as I can, to tell them they can get back up, and make my way to the seat next to Robert. Jocelyn sits at a nearby table, and there's a place for Mother next to me.

Andries and Reginald are already here as well, sitting on the other side of Mother's chair. They both look stately, but it's Andries who really surprises me. I didn't know he could clean up this well. I'm used to seeing him when he's going over artifacts and not when he's attending a formal dinner. Even at the funeral, he wasn't this cleaned up. He must have remembered Constance in the way she'd have liked best, and not in the way the world would expect.

The other guards are waiting nearby. They are unobtrusive, but comforting to have around. Not that I don't like having them here, but I do wish they didn't need to be. The thought of Captain Smythe hanging around, waiting to attack, isn't a pleasant one.

The meal is held until Mother arrives, but fresh apple juice is served while we wait. I'd forgotten how crisp it tastes.

"This is delicious," Robert says.

"Everything here made from apples is fresh," I respond. "It makes it all the better."

"You've been here before, then?"

"Yes, but it was a long time ago. I don't remember much, other than the tasty apples."

His expression falls. "I was hoping you'd be able to remember a little more."

"I remember more," Reginald says. "I was here recently, at the service of the king and queen."

"Do you remember anything useful?" Robert asks.

I want to groan. Perhaps Reginald does know something of interest, but I'm expecting a long lecture that somehow leads back to humans.

"Oh, yes. Of course I remember a lot. The apples here are like nothing else in the world. But you see, they make more than one type of apple. Just like there are humans and elves, there are different apples. Unlike apples, we and the humans are always sweet." He laughs, like it's some kind of joke.

"But like the apples, we all have skin," he continues, "and thoughts and feelings hidden on the inside. Though our thoughts and feelings aren't the same, person to person or elf to elf. Humans are such interesting creatures. I don't know how they get by without a little magic here and there to help them out. Despite my studies, I find it difficult to understand. They do have technology, though, which we don't."

His talking continues, but I stop listening and instead watch those from the village gathering around to eat. They seem very patient and excited to be here. They watch our table with eager gazes, though they don't make eye contact with me. I don't know if it's because of my looks or my status, or that they haven't even thought about it.

Reginald finally stops talking. I turn to Robert, feeling suddenly shy. I keep my voice down but know that Reginald still might be able to hear me. "I just realized, I don't even know your favorite food."

"Lamb chops," he says with a smile. "You?"

"It's hard to pick a favorite. It used to be anything that Constance made." The memory makes my chest ache. "What's your favorite color?"

"I can't decide if it's brown or blue."

Realizing he's talking about my eyes that are brown around the irises and blue tinting the edges, I look down.

"What's your favorite color?" His voice is warm.

"Golden brown, of course."

He smiles. We continue trading favorite things until Mother finally arrives, a servant announcing her. She comes in with a flourish, her voluminous skirt flowing around her. All rise and bow to her. She moves among the people and finds her seat before having them sit again. It's very ceremonial. More than this little town must be accustomed to.

Once everyone regains their seats, dinner is finally started. There's enough food for everyone here and then some. The people have been most generous with their food, though in a town that does nothing but grow food, it mustn't be that hard. I appreciate it still. The pork is my favorite, a delectable combination of savory and sweet apples.

As the meal winds down, people come forward to speak with me or Mother. They are a happy people, tan from working in the fields, though their skin is still not quite as dark as most humans.

A little girl in particular comes up with her mother and can't stop staring at Robert. I can't blame her. All I want to do is stare, too.

"What is it?" I ask her.

"Why are his ears shaped so funny?"

Her mother shushes her as I look at the little girl's ears that arc into fine points. Perfect little elf ears.

"It's fine," Robert says. "My ears are shaped like this because I'm a human. Have you ever seen a human before?"

The little girl shakes her head, still not taking her wide-eyed gaze from him.

"Well, now you can tell all your friends that you have."

The girl finally looks at me. "Does that mean she's almost a human? Her ears look like they want to be like yours."

Heat rushes to my face. I'm grateful when Robert answers for me. "She is the most beautiful elf in all the world, but she's trying to help humans and elves do more together, part of which is by having ears like that."

The girl's eyes grow wider. "Wow."

The mother hurries the girl along. I continue to greet people in line, but Robert's words stick with me. They warm part of me, but the rest isn't so sure. If he's right, why won't my own mother look at me?

AFTER THE CROWD'S NOISE dies down, Robert, Jocelyn and I go for a walk through the orchards.

She stays behind us, acting as chaperone but giving us a chance to spend time with one another uninterrupted. After the carriage ride here, it's most welcome.

I don't know what to do with Robert. I want to take his hand, but memories of Abner float to the surface. He said he wanted Robert and me to get married, but it's hard to imagine that I get Robert when I should have Abner. What's worse is that they were best friends.

"What are you thinking about?" Robert asks.

I glance at him, wondering if he can read minds and doesn't like where my thoughts are going. "What are you thinking?"

He lifts an eyebrow but doesn't protest my steering the conversation to him. "I'm thinking it's a good day for mitchen."

"What's that?" I've never heard of such a thing.

"It's a sport. You don't play it over here?"

I shake my head. "Not that I know. How do you play?"

"Ideally there'd be more people, but the two of us can practice catching the ball." He reaches up and picks an apple off the tree. I expect him to bite into it. Instead, he lobs it at me.

I catch it more by reflex than anything else.

"Good job," he says.

I hold the apple in the air. "What am I supposed to do with it now? And do you always play with apples?"

"Usually it's a ball, a little bigger than an apple. Throw it back to me."

I toss it to him, and it goes off to the side, but he catches it. A nervous giggle escapes me. "Sorry."

"Don't be."

We toss the apple back and forth several times—my aim not improving—while he tells me about the sport of mitchen. It's an easy afternoon, one I wouldn't expect to have after the difficulties we faced on our travels.

I finally manage to deliver the apple right to him.

"Nice one," he says.

I grin, a strange sort of pleasure rising within me.

He strides over to me and says, "I've been thinking... Maybe we should hire Captain Zaccheus for our honeymoon. We could stay on his ship all day."

Talk of our honeymoon makes my cheeks heat. "Unless pirates come."

"There is that. What do you want to do for our honeymoon, then?"

My thoughts turn to Abner, the one I planned to have a honeymoon with. When I first met him, I avoided him, but as I got to know him, I wouldn't have minded traveling with him. It's odd to think of doing so with someone else, even if it's the man I love. "I don't know. Something relaxing."

"Are you all right? You seem a little distant."

I clear my throat, trying to push away my fears. It doesn't work. "Honestly, Robert, I'm scared. This is a new life for us. I'm not sure what to think of it. I want it, but..."

He holds still. "But what?"

Do I tell him? It feels strange to open up like this, but he's going to be my husband. I have to get used to communicating with him. "Lots of things. I don't know what's going to happen to the two of us. I worry about Captain Smythe being out there and having to wonder if he's going to capture me again. Torture me or those I care about." I look down at my fingers. "And I worry that you'll think of me differently, since I was growing to care for Abner. Not the way I do for you, but I was beginning to think of him as a friend."

"That's what you're worried about?"

I nod.

Next thing I know, I'm wrapped in his arms. "First, I'm glad you found Abner to be a friend," he says. I know he wasn't always... nice to you, but he really was a great guy. It makes me happy that you saw that about my best friend. I miss him like nothing else, and to know you miss him a little bit too makes me feel like we're together in this. Understand?"

"Yes." My reply is muted by his shirt.

"Now, about Captain Smythe... I don't know what's going to happen with him. I'd like to think he'll leave us alone, but I will always be there for you. I won't let him take you again."

His words send a wave of relief through me. Knowing he's on my side, that we can be a team, holds reassurance.

It feels so good to be in his arms. Being safe with him. Not that I can't protect myself, but I don't have to do it alone.

When we part, I glance around to find Jocelyn facing the other direction. Mother wouldn't approve of her chaperoning job, but I appreciate it.

"You have a good friend," Robert says, looking in the same direction as me.

"I have the best of friends." I gaze at him, hoping he knows I mean him too.

"Arabella?"

It sounds so good hearing my name come from his lips.
"Yes?"

"I want you to know that I love you."

"I love you too."

We're in this together, no matter what.

Chapter
TEN

~

WE'RE ALL GATHERED together in a meeting room at the inn. Everyone except Mother. Even Reginald came. I shouldn't be surprised, but I am a little disappointed. I hoped he'd decide to sleep in. I'm not amazed by mother not coming, though I wanted her to. She's more of a sleep-in elf than a hands-on elf. She'll do her duty more when she wakes, I'm sure. Until then, I have Jocelyn to chaperone me.

This room too is made out of all dark wood but lit up by a multitude of windows. For being one of the oldest buildings in the community, it's well taken care of; that much is clear. If the rest of the village is too, maybe there's still hope for the scrolls.

"Where do we start?" I ask no one in particular. When no one replies, I look to Andries.

"I don't know," he says. "This town is unfamiliar to me. I'm not sure what to expect at all."

"Is there anyone here that's an expert in the village's history, like Andries is?" Robert says. "Someone we could ask and get information from?

I shrug. I don't know the people here that well. I realized this would be hard, but I didn't think I wouldn't even know where to start.

"Don't look at me," Reginald says. "My expertise is in humans."

I refrain from rolling my eyes and telling him no one was looking at him.

"I could go around and ask the locals what they know of this town," Andries says. "See if someone can point me to any ancient ruins. If not, I'll ask to be shown around. I know the history here quite well already, but I'm certain there's still a lot I can learn."

"That sounds like a good place to start," I say.

Andries stands. "Why don't you join me, Reginald? It's about time you learned a little more about elves."

Reginald looks aghast, but silently follows Andries out the room. Thank goodness he does so. I don't know how much I can stand of him. It's rude of me to think it, but it's hard not to, when he's so adsorbed in humans.

"And I think we should check out the library," Robert says. "There's bound to be some information there."

"This is going to be more work than I thought." I should have studied a map before we left to look for ancient ruins. I guess I thought if something was here, we'd stumble onto it like I stumbled onto the scroll in the cave.

"I'm afraid so," Robert says.

I leave a note with Catarrha to give to my mother when she rises for the day. Together, Robert, Jocelyn, and I walk to the library with a few guards. It's not far from the inn, and it's a pretty path too, with trees on both sides of the road—though not apple trees. The air has a fresh, clean aroma to it. I'm almost sad to walk in the library, but I can't help but hope there is something helpful inside.

The scent of books fills the air. The library is vast, full to the brim with books everywhere the eye can see, even some on the floor, which pains me. The rows don't always make sense, turning here and there. Perhaps to the librarian it's all in order, but all I see is a lot of mess we're going to have to wade through to find anything useful. The shelves aren't even straight. They jut out in odd places.

I shake my head, and we move farther in until we find the librarian.

He has his gray hair down around his shoulders and a pencil stuck behind one of his thinly pointed ears.

"Hello, I am Princess Arabella. We were wondering if you'd be able to help us."

He gives a bow. "I'd be happy to, Princess. What do you need?"

"Do you know where we can find any information about an old scroll? We're interested in finding out more of the history of our land, specifically, any scrolls with that information," I say.

"What type of old scroll?" he asks. "We have a lot to choose from."

That's the opposite of what I want to hear. "We're looking for one that's about the history of humans and elves, or one that could point us to where such a scroll might be found in this town."

"Well, you've come to the right place. Pomum Heart is one of the oldest towns in Omanska. We keep good records here. Let me show you the area of the library that holds the oldest recorded documents."

We follow him through stacks and stacks of books until the leather bound tomes give way to scrolls. We take several more turns, and I'm beginning to feel lost.

"You should find what you're looking for in one of these five rows." The librarian points to each row as he walks by, and my heart sinks. The rows are busting with scrolls, more than I've ever seen in one place before. When he said they keep good records, he meant they keep a lot of them, not that they keep their records in good order.

"Is there anything else I can do for you?" he asks.

"Is there some method of filing we could use, to find what we want?" I respond.

"I'm afraid not. We put all our records here, but I've never had time to organize them. There's too much to do and only me to do it."

I share a glance with Robert.

"That's all we need for the moment, then," Robert says. "Thank you."

With a little bow, the librarian walks away, leaving the three of us alone.

I don't know how we're going to find anything in here. "This is a much bigger task than looking for a cave."

Robert raises his eyebrows while glancing over the shelves. "You can say that again."

"If we all work together, maybe it won't be so bad," Jocelyn says.

A voice of hope in all this madness. We'll need a lot more than that, I'm afraid. "It will make the job somewhat easier," I reply. "We should all wear gloves doing this job. Andries says otherwise we can damage the scrolls. Why don't we start searching through the stacks?"

"And I'll make myself scarce over here in this stack while you two should start on the other end," Jocelyn says with a wink.

"I'll help her," one of the guards says. The other guards wait outside.

"Thank you." I feel my cheeks heat but don't really mind it this time. Not with just Jocelyn and Robert around to witness it.

"Just don't tell your mother it was my idea," Jocelyn says.

I giggle. At least some good is coming from all of this. More alone time with Robert is exactly what I want, though we won't get a chance to do or say much of anything because we'll be too busy looking. But we'll be together.

The search is interesting at first. I make certain to put each scroll back where I find it after I've concluded it's nothing I need. The problem is none of them offers the slightest hint.

Scrolls about how many babies were born each year. Scrolls about crops. Scrolls about the jobs around town. Scrolls about schooling. Scrolls about taking stock of apples—a lot of scrolls about apples. There may be some interesting stuff buried in here somewhere, but so far not the interesting stuff we're looking for.

We search for hours with no luck. Scroll after scroll after scroll. It's the most hopeless task I've ever undertaken. My eyes are weary of all the looking, but we can't stop. We have to go on until we find something.

The time continues to pass as the scrolls I've looked at grow more, though the ones I still need to check are mountainous. How are we ever going to check these all?

"Any luck?" I ask Robert.

"None."

"Perhaps Jocelyn is doing better than we are?"

"She gave us privacy, and we're only using it to search for things." He walks over to me and wraps his arms around me.

I lean into him, resting my head on his shoulder. "I hope we do find something," I say. "It seems like an important piece of history."

"I hope we do too."

"How long do you think we should look before we call it off?" I ask. "There's so much here. It could take years to go through it all. I don't want to put our wedding off for too long."

He pulls me closer. "Me neither. I'm eager to make you my wife."

I look up at him. "Your wife. I like the sound of that."

My chest warms as my pulse speeds up. I lean in closer, unable to take my gaze from his lips. This is it. The moment I've been waiting for. Our first kiss. He seems anxious for it too, bending down to meet me.

There's a scuffling sound.

"What was that?" I pull away from our almost kiss with a silent curse.

"I didn't hear anything," Robert says.

"Hmm… I could have sworn I heard something." I glance back up at him wishing the noise hadn't happened. It feels as if we missed our moment. Plus, now I'm on edge. Not exactly how I imagined my first kiss. I duck my head, wondering if there's a way to get the moment back. "Where else do you think we should search?"

He sighs. "I don't know. This place is a maze."

"Some libraries are."

"Could the scrolls be hiding in here somewhere?" he asks.

"It seems as good a place as any. Maybe someone found them and didn't know what exactly they were, so they left them here. We should get more people helping and start organizing this all. It'll go a lot faster with help."

"Sounds like a good plan to me." He cocks his head to the side. "I think I heard something now."

"Me, too." I pull out my sword. As soon as he realizes what I'm doing, he follows my lead.

"You think it's trouble?" I ask.

"The way my life has gone lately, I always think it's trouble."

"Fair enough, but I hope it isn't."

The noise grows closer—a faint type of scratching that grows louder as it approaches. A moment later, a mouse scurries by.

"That is disgusting," I say.

"Old library, I guess," he says, putting his sword away. "They should take better care of their stuff. Aren't you going to sheathe your blade?"

"Not if I can use it to get rid of that rat."

He chuckles.

"I'm serious," I say.

"That's what makes it so funny." He moves closer. "When we're old, I can still see you clutching your sword and chasing after rats."

I laugh. "If there are vermin in our home, we'll have bigger problems than my running around with a sword."

He wraps an arm around my waist and pulls me closer. "What type of problems would those be?"

There's a loud crash, and the bookcase collapses. Robert jumps away, holding the bookshelves from falling all the way down on me. Scrolls tumble around, landing all over my body.

"Get out of here," Robert shouts.

"Guards," I call. Though I fear my voice gets lost in the vastness of the building. I run away toward the exit where the guards should be, dodging the falling scrolls only to come out to face a scraggly-looking stinky man holding a sword.

"What are you doing in here?" I yell.

He grins, half of his teeth missing. "Trying to kill your betrothed."

I thrust my blade toward him. "No one hurts Robert."

He parries and jumps backward. I run at him full force, but trip over scrolls and fall on my butt. My assailant takes the opportunity to sneak past me, heading for Robert.

More men come running in, all as ragged as the first. *Pirates.* They swarm in so fast, it's hard to keep track of them, but I count four more as I gain my feet.

I glance back at Robert. He's holding his own against the first pirate. I stand firm between him and the rest.

They come at me all at once. I swing my sword so fast, its blade is a blur. Instinct carries me on. They press in on me, and I hurry backward, blocking their advance. My calves bump into something. The bookshelf. Where did Robert go?

I jump over the bookshelf, turn tail, and run. Robert's at the other side of the fallen bookshelf, fighting the toothless man. The man's back is to me as he viciously attacks Robert. Though Robert is holding his own, I don't mind giving him a little help, especially when we have more pirates coming.

I bash the back of the man's head with the hilt of my sword as hard as I can. He falls to the ground. With a quick tuck and roll, I come to a standing position next to Robert.

"Are you all right?" he asks.

"For the moment."

But more men are coming at us. The first one falls, hitting his head as he goes down the bookshelf. The other three follow behind but more slowly.

This is it. Here they come.

They jump off the bookshelf and come at us with their swords. Robert and I fight back, working in motion together.

There's a gasp. I look up to see Jocelyn, a guard right beside her.

"Get help," I yell.

The attackers look at her. One breaks off from the group and tries for her and the guard. I swipe at his legs and connect. He falls to the ground. I hope that's enough of a head start for Jocelyn to get help because Robert is fighting two people at once. He needs assistance.

I turn toward the closest attacker and thrust my sword toward him. He slashes at me but then trips over a scroll and falls flat on his face. I put my blade to his neck. A second sword comes and knocks mine away, letting the fallen man get back up. The second attacker leaves Robert to try to help his partner.

Robert and I go at both of them. Soon, the guard joins us. The pirates turn and run, picking up their fallen comrade on the way. I move to pursue, but Robert stops me.

"Jocelyn will get help. This one is waking up," he says.

"Fantastic." I rush to where Robert is holding the point of his sword over the attacker's throat. When will Captain Smythe give up on attacking us and leave us alone?

The pirate stirs and then comes all the way to with a jump, but Robert holds his sword steady.

"Why are you trying to kill Prince Robert?" I demand.

The pirate laughs.

I add my blade to his throat. "Why are you trying to kill him?"

"You're smart. Why don't you figure it out?"

"Do you have a death wish?"

"I don't, which is why I'm not saying more than that. Captain Smythe is more likely to kill me than you."

I press my sword harder into his skin, but he's right; I won't kill him. I won't stoop to Captain Smythe's level and torture him.

I thrust my sword away from his neck, disgusted. "You can rot in prison, then. I'm certain you'll find it comfortable there."

Robert takes him by the arm. "It's time for you to go to jail."

"Will that be enough to stop Captain Smythe, though?" I ask.

The pirate laughs. I guess I have my answer.

Chapter
ELEVEN

~

THE REST OF THE GUARDS show up too late for the fight. They passed no one on the way in, but one of them later found an open window we think they went through. Some of my guards follow their trail, hoping to catch up to them.

The rest of my guards escorts us back to the inn. I'm still jittery after the incident. I can't believe they're coming after both Robert and me now. Nowhere seems safe.

A guard goes to inform my mother what happened. I dread her reaction, and I'm grateful that it doesn't happen in front of me. As long as she lets us keep searching. We get word from Andries that he's still searching the town but has found nothing yet.

The other guards return hours later saying they lost the trail. There were some villagers who saw them, but once they were out of the town, there was no hope for catching them. I give them all a smile and tell them to take a break while the others watch over us. I know they tried. It's just this Captain Smythe is so sneaky.

Robert, Jocelyn, and I meet together in a conversing room. One guard stands at the door and one at the window. More wait in the hall. The room is small enough to be cozy, but large enough that more people could come in if needed. I hope no one else comes by, though. I'm tired, and my nerves are taut. I'm not certain how well I could handle extra company.

"Are you certain you're both all right?" Jocelyn asks.

"I'm fine," I say and look to Robert.

"No harm done," he says. "Except the mess in the library."

I groan. "It was hard enough going through every scroll before. How are we going to do it now?"

"Maybe the place won't be so bad after the librarians get to it."

I don't say it, but seeing how the librarians took care of the library before, I can't see them fixing it up very well after what happened during the fight.

"Besides, I wasn't having any luck," Jocelyn says. "Were you two?"

"None," I say. "There was nothing but boring factual pieces. Nothing on the real history."

"That's what I found too," Robert says.

"I'm not certain we're looking in the right area," I say. "Though I'm not sure where else we could look. If the librarian thought the information would be there, it doesn't seem likely that we'll find it somewhere else."

"Perhaps it's not in the library," he says.

"Wherever it is," I say, "we have to keep looking. I have hope it's out there still." Although it's not as much hope as before.

"Maybe Andries was able to find something," Jocelyn says.

We fall into silence while I think on the possibility. He may have found something, but after the luck we've had, I can't say I'm expecting it. I exchange a glance with Robert. He seems to be thinking the same thing, though neither of us wants to say it.

"I think I'll give you two some alone time," she says, "but since your mother's in the same building, I'll stay in the corner if that's all right."

"You don't need to, but it's really appreciated," I say. "Thank you so much, Jocelyn."

She moves as far from us as possible and begins doing needlework. I don't know how she can do such delicate work after chasing off pirates. It left me too jumpy to do anything of the sort. At least someone here has steady hands.

Robert scoots his chair closer to mine. "You did a wonderful job, handling that pirate."

It's kind of him to say, but not all true. "More like let my temper get the best of me. All this time they've been trying to kidnap me, to stop the wedding. Now they want you dead instead."

He's silent a moment. When he speaks, it's with a hesitance I haven't heard before. "They're trying to take my life. But they'd been trying to kill Abner since the betrothal."

"What?" Fear and anger mix inside me in a nervous combination.

"It's true. It's one reason he and I pretended to be sailors when we met you. He was sick of having his life threatened all the time."

"Like yours is now?"

"Yes. The pirates seem pretty intent on taking me out."

"Do you think it's the wedding, or something else?"

"It has to be the wedding. I didn't have problems when I was third in line for the throne and we weren't engaged."

I worry for him. For us. "What are we going to do about it?"

He leans forward and wraps his arms around me. It feels so good to finally have him be able to do things like this after wanting him to for so long.

"We'll keep living," he says. "We can't let them bring us down."

"But when both our lives are threatened now, do you think it will get better when we're actually married? Or are we going to have to deal with this the rest of our lives?"

"I don't know." He slowly pulls away. "I can believe it will go away when the pirates realize they've failed, but if it doesn't, we'll keep doing what we always do. Fight back those who try to harm us and show everyone else that we are united. We'll have two armies behind us. We'll find a way around them."

I squeeze his hand. "I suppose you're right." I have to believe things will go as well as we hope.

Chapter
TWELVE

~

MY THOUGHTS ARE HEAVY as I move throughout the library. Others are searching all around, and I should be doing the same. The problem is I'm worried about Robert's life being in danger. Even with our guards around, it doesn't seem enough. If pirates could get to us before, why not again? I tell myself our guards will be enough. We've fought them off before. We can do it again. But the worry remains.

I stumble through scrolls on the ground. I should pick them up, look them over, and place them back on the shelves that have been propped back up for that purpose, but I feel too numb. Too overcome by everything. What was the point of coming here? Are we going to find a hint of something? It feels less and less likely.

A shadow appears at the end of the aisle, and I put my hand on the hilt of my sword. The shadow moves closer until it rounds the bend. *Emeline.* I relax and take my hand off my sword, but knowing her, I stay ready to grab it at a moment's notice. I may have accepted her apology, but that doesn't mean I trust her.

She curtsies. "I was told I would find you here."

"And you did." I keep my voice civil, but I'm tired of everything. I'm not in the mood to deal with much today. "What can I do for you?"

"I was wondering if I could help."

"Help?" The word is foreign, coming from her. Unless it means helping to give me to one of my enemies. She did look serene before, but after seeing her and then being attacked shortly after, it has my suspicions on edge.

"Yes, with your search. I don't know what you're looking for exactly, but if you tell me, I can provide another set of eyes."

"Forgive me. That's not what I expected." Not even close.

She twists her hands together and glances down at them. "I know you must not think much of me. I certainly haven't given you reason to, but if you give me the opportunity to help, I'd like to try to change that."

Change. She seems to have, but has she really? I suppose there's only one way to know for certain. "Do you remember the scroll we found in the caves on Sulamay Island?"

"I do. We were hiding from the pirates when you knocked over the vase it was in."

"Yes, well, that scroll led us to another one, on Bardus. It seems whoever wrote them has a good knowledge of part of our history and our people. The second scroll we found directed us here. We're trying to find a third scroll that will hopefully give us more information on our heritage."

"I see. That's something I can help with," she says. "What type of scroll am I looking for?"

"Something very, very old. Something that talks of our history and has to do with humans and elves."

"I'll get right on it."

It's hard to trust her with the task, but let's face it, we need all the help we can get. "If you have any questions you can ask me or Andries."

She nods and then picks up a scroll from the ground. She looks at it and says, "What do I do with the ones that aren't what we're looking for?"

"Put them back on the shelf."

"Don't the librarians want them in a particular order?"

"They said this area of the library has never been organized. Part of the reason we're having such a hard time finding anything."

"It seems a little odd to do that, but—" She shrugs and places the scroll on the nearest shelf.

I pick up a scroll by my feet, more to feel like I'm doing something other than watching her than because I think it will contain anything. Everything here is useless. Does it matter how many eggs a chicken laid in a certain year? Maybe to some, but not to me. It doesn't help me learn if there's a way to do a better job of bringing us and humans together.

I put the useless scroll on the shelf and look for the next one. Emeline seems to do the same. In fact, she's moving faster than me, doing a good job of going through all these scrolls. I can't imagine her doing this unless she meant what she said.

My first instinct, to believe her, was correct. This place may have been as good for her as my parents thought it would be. After how she betrayed me, I never thought I'd see the day of her reform. I should use this chance to get to know her—something I never got to do when she was my servant. If I had, things might be different.

"Tell me, Emeline," I say, "how did you come to work at the castle?"

"My mother was a servant before she married my father and had me. She always talked about the castle like it was some magical place. I thought it would be, when I went off at eleven to get a job there."

"But it wasn't magical. Was it?" I ask, knowing the answer.

"Nothing is magical about scrubbing out chamber pots." She laughs. "There was good food on the table. That was hard to find at home."

"Why was that?"

"Because my mother had a difficult time finding work, and my father didn't get paid much, working at a local stable. I think that's why I wanted so badly for the castle to be a magical place."

"I wish it was." I know from growing up there it was anything but. It doesn't mean I had it harder than Emeline, though. "What happened to your parents?"

"They both died, several years ago."

I stop looking at the scroll in my hand. "I'm sorry to hear that."

She shrugs. "While I miss them, they were gone for some time for me, before they actually passed away. I didn't usually go see them on my day off, so it could be months and months between visits."

"Is that why you were so set on helping Octavian?" I make myself ask.

She thinks a moment. "I suppose that played a part. He did give me attention like I never had before. I guess I just wanted it to be real. I wanted to know someone could care about me that way. I'd fallen for Octavian, and it bothered me that he wouldn't marry me. I'm sorry. I was jealous and resentful."

"I'm sorry you had to find that in him. I'm sorry I couldn't be the one to boost your confidence."

She waves me off. "It's partly my fault for not reaching out to you like Jocelyn did. Besides, you have a lot of things on your mind. You have a whole kingdom you'll someday rule. They need you more than I do."

"I'm still sorry."

"Thank you for that." She opens another scroll and looks at it. "There aren't many useful scrolls in here. I wonder why they keep them all around."

"Probably because no one is crazy enough to go through them like we are."

"You know, that makes perfect sense."

We get back to work, with a few comments here and there. I feel glad we had this talk. Hopefully, things keep improving between us. It's hard to think she's the same girl who betrayed me. I guess there's hope for everyone.

Chapter
THIRTEEN
॰◡॰

THE NEXT DAY ROBERT, Jocelyn, Andries, and I enter the library together, our guards close by. Emeline had to work at the orphanage today. Andries never found out anything further from the town. Nothing was old enough to be from the same time period as the scrolls. It just has to be in the library. I feel in it in my gut. We'll find it.

We stop to talk to the librarian. Whatever he has to say will be better than going through more scrolls about nothing.

"Have you thought of anything else that may be useful to us?" Andries asks him.

"I'm afraid not," the librarian says. "We've never kept records like we should."

"Perhaps it's time to change that," I say. "The history of our people is more important than crop yields, after all."

He sighs. "I know. You're right. It's just that nobody has ever been interested. Well, except Granny Mae."

"Who's Granny Mae?" I ask.

"She's the oldest resident in town. She's always loved keeping notes on things and telling stories. She's something of a storyteller. If you go see her, you'd better be prepared to stay a long time. She does love chatting something much."

"Where does she—"

An explosion comes from somewhere in the library.

Robert grabs me by the hand and pulls me toward him. The smell of smoke permeates the air. Someone screams.

"We have to put out the fire," the librarian yells. "It will ruin everything."

"We can help," Robert says, keeping a tight grip on me. "Jocelyn, alert the villagers that we need help putting out a fire."

She hurries out of the library.

"Where's the fire at?" I ask with a niggling feeling.

"It's coming up ahead from the left," the librarian says, already hurrying off.

"I don't think this is a good idea," one of the guards says.

"We're going and sticking together, so it's safe," I say.

We follow the librarian, keeping up with his brisk pace through the stacks of books. I put my handkerchief to my nose. Though there's no fire in sight, there's a thin line of smoke above us. If it gets much worse, we'll have to turn back.

We go through the stacks, the way all too familiar. My heart drops when we spot the fire. It's spreading over the scrolls we were searching through. If what we need was there, it's now gone for good.

The flames aren't as bad as I expected but still enough to do untold damage.

I try to cast a spell, pulling water from the air to the fire, but there's not much moisture to be had in here. Under normal circumstances, that's a good thing for the books, but right now it's desperately needed. I try to stifle the air, but it's not within my powers to do.

The flames grow bright. Robert pulls at my arm and takes me back toward the exit. In what seems like no time at all but is much too long to let the fire burn, the villagers are gather, buckets in hand.

We run to the back of the line at a well, where villagers leave their empty buckets before racing toward the burning library. A male elf is filling buckets with water from the well. I grab one, readying it for him as soon as he's finished with the previous one.

"Stay here and help," Robert says. "I'm going to do what I can."

I nod, no words making it past my scratchy throat. A small bit of smoke inhalation is nothing compared to the devastation done inside the library.

My arms soon grow sore from passing buckets full of water down the line, but that doesn't stop me. Nothing will, until the fire is put out.

My mind races while I move my hands automatically. What could have caused such an explosion? Was it another attempt or Robert's life? How extensive is the damage? I can't worry about it. I'm doing the best I can, not to, but my mind rolls through such thoughts anyway.

After what seems like forever, word comes back that the fire is out. The villagers rub their arms, eyes heavy with loss.

Not caring that I'm sore as well, I hurry back to the library to see if something can be salvaged. I make my way past the villagers and through the building that still has a light cloud of smoke. My footsteps don't seem to go fast enough as I make my way to the place where the fire started.

When I get there, I find Robert with the librarian and Andries. The librarian moves to stomp on a burning scroll on the ground. Most everything in this section is gone. Some smoke damaged the other areas, but it's mostly contained here. All that's left is black and tattered pages, damaged with water. It's one of the saddest sights I've ever seen.

"All the scrolls are ruined," I say.

"I know," Robert responds.

Andries walks through the destroyed scrolls, his face white. "Who could have done this?"

It's then I realize the explosion was on purpose. Someone destroyed the scrolls we were looking for.

"Why would they have done it?" I ask. "It's not like we were looking for something that would harm anyone."

The librarian puts out the last of the flames.

"What caused the fire do you think?" I ask.

"I don't know," Robert says. "I only know whoever did it must have something against us."

Footsteps hurry our way, and Jocelyn comes into view. She did her job. She got the villagers, and we put out the fire.

But it's too late. The damage is already done.

Chapter
FOURTEEN

❧

I T'S A DISMAL DAY as we help the librarian clean out the charred mess. With the section of library we needed being destroyed, we should be heading home, but I can't bring myself to go yet—to admit defeat, though defeated we are. If someone destroyed the scrolls, they must have been there. That, or Robert's life is in danger, which is even more unacceptable.

My hands are black with soot. It's a good thing my mother is back at the inn. Today she's meeting with people from around the community, helping them with what she can and giving them her support. She wouldn't support my getting so dirty. I'll have to sneak back in my room to clean up before she sees me. It's worth it, though. Doing something is better than sitting around, thinking how everything we were searching through was ruined.

Now we'll never know the full truth of our history.

It's just as well. I should be focusing on my upcoming wedding.

Robert seems as upset by the loss as I am.

As I begin working on cleaning up the mess, just for something to do, the librarian stops me. "You don't need to do such work."

"I don't mind it."

"If you're sure?"

"I'm positive."

"What do we do now?" I ask Robert when the librarian goes off to find more cleaning supplies.

"I don't know. Maybe it's time we give up on it. Time we head back to Amara."

The thought haunts me. "It probably is. There's not much for searching now. I feel like we lost something. Like we can't continue on as we need to without it."

"We can stay longer if you want. Keep searching."

Oh, how I want to, but looking over this pile of mess left behind, the only thing to do is clean up. It really is time to move on. To get married. I wonder what we're going to miss out on from the destruction of that scroll. I should be happier about getting married, but I just feel at a loss.

"You're probably right," I tell him. "It's time to move on."

He takes my hand. "I know this isn't easy. We should have found it, too. It should never have been destroyed."

"I wish we could perceive who destroyed it. And why."

"That would be good information. I can't imagine anyone doing such a thing. Other than a pirate, that is."

"You think it was the pirate? But this seems a little strange of an action for them. They've concentrated on kidnapping me or killing you so far. Why would they destroy something we're looking for?"

He runs a hand through his hair. "It's only a guess, but I'm thinking we were supposed to be in that blast."

Fear strikes through me. "You really think so?"

"I do. If we hadn't stopped to speak with the librarian, we would have been amongst those shelves when the blast went off."

My throat is thick with what could have happened. "It's true. We'd have already been searching."

He gives my hand a squeeze. "But we weren't. Whoever it was didn't get us."

"But they're going to keep trying, especially if it's the pirates. They'll never give up."

"We'll have to capture Captain Smythe, then."

If only it was that simple.

WE MAKE OUR WAY BACK to the inn. I feel depressed by the turn of events. I also can't help but wonder when we'll be attacked again. It could be at any moment. Maybe the next turn will have pirates hiding. Or another explosion. So many bad things could happen.

Then again, so many good things can happen as well. I have to remember that. No matter how dark things get, I have people in my life who love me and care about me. As long as we can all stay safe, everything will be fine.

We reach the inn safely, much to my relief. We go in, wash up, and find my mother in the courtyard speaking with some of the villagers. We wait until she finishes before going up to her.

"You've returned so soon?" she asks.

I clench my teeth and take a deep, steadying breath. What happened today isn't something I want to think about or explain, but it needs to be explained.

Before I can say anything, Robert beats me to it. "There was an explosion at the library. As you can see, we're fine, but all the scrolls are ruined."

The skin around Mother's eyes wrinkles, if only for a second. The news is as upsetting to her as it is to us, even if she has a harder time showing it. "Did everyone come out as well? Was anything else damaged?"

"As far as we can tell, no one was harmed," he says. "A few other items were damaged, but mostly it was the older scrolls. We lost a lot of history."

She's quiet a moment before saying, "Come here, Arabella."

I move next to her, wondering what she could want of me.

She stands, and though she still doesn't look at me, her expression is tender. "I'm sorry you had to lose this opportunity. I know you were trying hard to find information about our past."

I sigh. "I was. It's lost now. Why would someone do that? That's all I want to know. Well, that and who did it."

"It's unfortunate that we didn't bring Stewart with us. He'd be able to give us a good idea, if not find the person himself."

"Maybe one of the other guards will be able to find out some information for us," Robert says.

"It's possible," Mother says. "None of them are as good at finding things as Stewart, but hopefully, they can come up with something."

"And what if they do find something?" I ask. "It's not like we can recover what was lost. We should try to find out because it could have cost us our lives, but I also think we should move on soon. Robert and I believe it's time to return and start planning the wedding."

"My dear girl," —Mother's voice cracks — "you have grown up so much." She sniffs and presses a handkerchief to the corners of her eyes. "I agree with you. It's time to return to Amara. Barring any difficulties, we shall be on the road tomorrow."

"What if we give it another day or two? Just to search… somewhere."

"It doesn't sound as if you even know where to search. If you did, maybe we could stay."

"You're right." I'm just disappointed that we never found any scrolls. More than disappointed.

But if we're going home, there is a bright spot. It's time to plan my wedding. Although I'm filled with bitter sweetness, now we've lost information I was hoping to gain, we can plan on something happy. Something joyous. Something I truly and dearly want.

I glance at Robert. He smiles that charming smile that melts my heart. I know this is it. This is what I've been waiting for. Finally, I'll be able to plan my wedding. And this time, it will be to the man I love.

Chapter

FIFTEEN

⌒

THAT EVENING WE'RE GATHERED around the table at the inn, eating dinner. Everyone is here. Andries, Mother, Jocelyn, Robert—even the guards are eating with us, though they're taking turns doing so. When it's not their turn to eat, they're standing guard, an awful reminder we're facing an enemy we don't fully understand. If we did, maybe we'd be able to stop them instead of constantly being threatened by them.

Some of the guard are even out combing the area for pirates. We've put on a massive search for them, even some of the town guard are helping, but no news of any yet. Either they left the area, or they're hiding somewhere very sneaky.

The meal is somber. Besides the burning in the library, no one was expecting to go home so soon. And though leaving means going to a wedding, it doesn't take away the pain of losing something so important. The pain of having something we were searching for destroyed... if it was even there to begin with.

I don't know why we came in the first place. We'd have been better off looking after we had the wedding. And we still can look after the wedding. It'll just take us some time to come back. Perhaps instead of waiting, I can put Emeline in charge of searching for it.

"It'll be all right," Robert whispers next to me.

I give him half a smile, all I can manage at the moment. "It will be. It didn't turn out like I planned. Nothing ever seems to."

"Hey, don't be hard on yourself. Things rarely turn out according to plan, but that doesn't mean they're going to be bad."

"I guess you're right. I wish we could have found the scroll. But we're going to be married soon." I smile wider, letting my love for him fill my heart.

"What are you two talking about?" my mother asks.

"The wedding," I say loud enough for everyone to here. "If we can't have our history, we can make our future."

"Well said." Jocelyn grins.

We finish the last of our meal in silence. Dessert is good, but I have to force it down. Any other time, it would be a delectable apple tart; now it's dry in my mouth.

Once I'm done, I give Robert's hand a squeeze—not caring that anyone can see it—give goodnights to everyone, and head off to bed. Jocelyn follows.

As soon as the door of our bedroom closes, I fling myself on the bed. "This is so much harder than I expected."

Jocelyn sits on the bed next to me. "What is? Leaving, or not finding the scroll?"

"Both. But mostly not finding it. That piece of history is lost forever if it was in the library. I keep telling myself it was nothing important anyway, but my heart says there is something to what it said."

"I wish that there was more we could do," she says.

I pull myself to a sitting position. "There's often not enough we can do."

"I know what you mean. It's been hard this whole journey, being unable to do more for you."

I turn to her and take in her eyes, glimmering with unshed tears. "What do you mean? You've done so much."

"Not really." She brushes the tears away quickly, like she is embarrassed about them. "The most I did was help get a carriage to pick you up after you fainted back in Derelinquo Fork. Even then, it was luck that we weren't found by someone with ill intents. I haven't done nearly enough while you've been going through so much." She glances down.

"That's not true." She's tortured because of me. She's been through more than anyone should ever have to go through. When she looks at me, I say, "You've always been there for me. Listened to me. Helped me. Lands, you were tortured. If it wasn't for you, I don't know what I would have done. Probably gone stark raving mad."

She gives an almost smile. "You would have survived."

"No. I wouldn't have made it this far without you. You believed in me when no one else would. You've been my rock through everything."

A tear slips down her cheek. "That's hard to remember when I still want to do so much."

"There's much I want to do still that I can't do either."

"You'll find a way to unite humans and elves," she says, "and I'll do whatever I can to help." Her words bring comfort, but no answers.

"Thank you. Your support means more than I can say."

"But we need more."

"I'm afraid that, yes, we do."

A new resolve enters her gaze. "Then we'll find a way. What about the woman the librarian talked about? Granny Mae?"

I forgot all about Granny Mae with the explosion. I should have remembered her, but she was only mentioned once in passing. She could be the key to finding the scroll, if it still exists.

A new hope sparks inside me—one I didn't believe possible, but is dimmed by reality. "That's a good idea. We should speak with her before we go. Only I'm afraid her stories may not be enough to give us the answers we're looking for." I just have to be realistic about this. My hopes have already been brought up once only to be let down. I don't want to go through that again.

"I know. She's not been around long enough to know personally about the scroll, but maybe she's heard something that can help."

"It's worth a try. It will only delay us a little," I say.

"The librarian did say she likes to talk a lot."

I sigh. "A whole day then, possibly."

"I know you're anxious to be married. I could stay and talk to her while you start making preparations for your wedding."

"You're a good friend, but it's only a day."

"Then we should we go?" she asks.

"First thing in the morning."

We hurry to get ready for bed. The chance of something happening tomorrow keeps me up, but more than that, it's the conviction we'll fail yet again that has me tossing and turning that night.

Chapter
SIXTEEN

∾

THE MORNING DAWNS bright and early. After a
fitful night's sleep, the last thing I want to do is get
up, but we have a lead to follow, as slim as it may be.
I send Jocelyn to tell the others where we're going and arrange
for guards while I gather food from the kitchens, both to feed
us and to take to Granny Mae. She may not need the food,
but it feels wrong to go asking questions without bringing
her something.

Jocelyn meets me out front by the carriage. "Done," she
says. "Prince Robert said he'll make arrangements for us to
leave tomorrow and will speak with your mother when she
wakes up."

"And I got the food. Let's go."

Several guards follow us to the library where we ask for
directions to Granny Mae's house. After a few minutes' walk,
we come across a cozy cottage, complete with flowers on the
windowsill and along the path leading to the front door.

Jocelyn knocks on the door, and a moment later, it opens.

A woman several years older than me, with shining red hair, stands before us. She curtsies, and I motion for her to rise. "How can I help you, Your Highness?" she asks.

"We were hoping to speak with Granny Mae," I say. "She may have information we need."

"I'm afraid she's not doing well. You can speak with her, but she's not always very coherent. Her time is growing near."

My small flicker of hope wanes. "We don't want to disturb her if she's not up for visitors."

The woman gives a small laugh. "She's always up for visitors. There's nothing she loves better in the world than to talk to people. Come on in. Maybe today will be a good day."

I turn to the guards. "Will you wait out here, please?"

"Yes, ma'am."

Jocelyn and I enter the house. It's as darling on the inside as it is on the outside. Gingham curtains hang at the windows, and fresh flowers sit in a white vase on a table. In the corner of the room, looking out the window, is an ancient elf. I've never seen so many wrinkles on anyone before, and her hair is the color of daisy petals.

She glances at the red haired woman, who hovers close by.

"Granny Mae," the woman says in a loud voice, "some very important people have come to speak with you. Are you up for visiting with them?"

"I'd love to," comes the surprisingly clear reply.

The other woman turns to us. "Be sure to speak loudly. She doesn't hear as well as she used to."

"I brought this for you." I hand her the basket of goodies. "Thank you for allowing us into your home."

Jocelyn and I take a seat on a small sofa to the side of Granny Mae, who turns her attention to us.

"And what can I do for two such pretty young girls?" Granny Mae asks.

My cheeks heat at her words. Compliments aren't something I hear anymore, except from Robert. The sweet old woman is probably losing her eyesight as well as her hearing. "We have a few questions for you," I say.

"Everyone has questions. It's all people think about anymore. Myself, I much prefer answers."

"That's good, because we're hoping you have some for us."

"Oh, I have lots of things to say. Whether it's the answer you're looking for or not is something else," she tells me. "You remind me of someone I used to know. I just can't think of who."

Her gaze is intense, and I try not to squirm under it. I've been under scrutiny before—this is nothing new—but there's something about it that has me wanting to lower my gaze anyway. "We're looking for an old scroll," I say.

"Oh, yes. Lots of those. My father used to be in charge of scrolls."

A zip of excitement races through me. Could he have known about the scroll we're looking for? "It had to do with humans and elves."

She moves her gaze back to the window. "What did?"

"The scrolls your father used to be in charge of."

When she faces me again, her eyes are clouded. "You remind me of someone I used to know. Who was it?"

I twist my hands within the skirt of my dress so I don't give away my frustration. "I'm not sure, but we're looking for a scroll. You're father might have known about it. It had to do with humans and elves."

"There's so much contention between the two races nowadays. I want to sit here in peace."

I'm convinced she knows something, but how do I get her to remember it? How do I get her to say what she knows? "We want peace, too. My best friend here is a human, while I'm an elf. We want nothing more than for our two races to give up this fighting."

Granny Mae rests her head on the back of her chair. The only sound is the creaking of her rocking chair as it slowly moves back and forth.

The woman who answered the door kneels down beside Granny Mae and puts her hand atop Granny's. "Mother, these women have come looking for answers to something very important. Do you remember anything about a scroll that had to do with humans and elves?"

"My father once met a pretty young elf. She was the most beautiful girl he ever laid eyes on. He was sure she'd never pay him any mind, but he decided to bring her flowers anyway. To his surprise, she loved the flowers and agreed to meet him formally. They courted and eventually fell in love enough to get married."

My heart sinks. Granny Mae is lost in her own world. There's no chance she'll remember something that probably happened hundreds of years before she was born. I sit back on the sofa, resigned to listen to this woman's stories, knowing that, if she has the answers we need, they're lost in a mind that's deteriorated beyond recall.

"What happened?" Jocelyn asks.

Granny focuses her gaze on her. "The girl's father disapproved, of course. My father was just a blacksmith, and the girl's father wanted so much more for her."

"So they never made it together?"

Her gaze clouds over once again. "Who?"

Her daughter stands and faces us. "I'm sorry. She's like this most days, now. It's hard to get a coherent thought out of her." She turns back to her mother. "What about the scrolls with the humans and elves? Do you remember anything about them?"

Granny Mae's eyes crinkle with confusion. "Who are you?"

"It's me—Jane. Your daughter."

"You can't be her. My daughter is a little girl."

Jane grips Granny Mae's hand and turns toward us, a sheen of tears in her eyes. "I'm sorry we couldn't be more helpful."

"It's all right," I say, though the disappointment is sharp. I didn't expect much coming here anyway, but still I hoped...

"Granny Mae," Jocelyn says scooting forward, "can you tell us what happened in the story of your father and the girl he fell in love with? Did the girl's father keep them separated?"

"Ah." Granny raises her eyebrows. "That's a story I haven't told in a long, long time. The girl was tired of being told what to do by her father. She longed to marry the one she loved, but she couldn't do it without her father's permission in that day."

"Did she earn it, somehow?" Jocelyn asks.

I hold back a sigh. If we aren't going to get any information from Granny, perhaps we should get going. Yet I don't want to be rude and leave in the middle of her story, especially if Jocelyn is asking for the rest of it. The tale is an interesting one. Forbidden love is something I'm familiar with, after all.

"Oh, she was a smart lass," Granny Mae continues. "She knew her father's love for her was great, but she also knew he might never approve of any marriage for her. No man was good enough—not in his eyes. She set out to show him all the good things the blacksmith could do. The way he could create things. Make something out of nothing. The way he incorporated magic into his work.

"Eventually her father saw his daughter would never be happy unless she married the blacksmith. Still, he didn't want to give up his only daughter. He devised a plan that would give the blacksmith a chance at his daughter's hand but would guarantee failure. An impossible task."

When she shifts her gaze toward the window once more, I'm afraid we've lost the story just when I was growing interested in it. "What was his plan?" I ask.

Granny Mae meets my gaze with surprising clarity. "Simple. If the blacksmith could create a hidden chamber within the library to protect the ancient scrolls, one that wouldn't be found by the enemy and would seal the scrolls until one worthy of reading them came forth, the girl's father would let them marry."

My heart pounds. A hidden chamber in the library? Is this what we've been searching for? Have we found it? "Did your father create it?"

She smiles. "Oh, yes. He made a hidden room within the library and then had the entire building rearranged, to make the room harder to find. Then he sealed up the ancient scrolls and won my mother's hand in marriage. The scrolls were said to have been about both humans and elves. That they contained a secret not many would believe."

"The scroll we've been looking for." It takes everything in me not to jump to my feet and run to the library. "And not one, but many."

"I think so, but perhaps not. My father didn't tell me the tale often. He was ashamed he couldn't win my mother's hand on his merits alone. When he told it, there was always a gleam in his eye that lead me to think there was more to the story than he was letting on. But he's long since passed. I'll never know for sure what that gleam was about."

I scoot forward in my seat and take both of Granny Mae's hands into my own. "Thank you for this story. You have done more than you know."

She nods with a heavy blink. "If you don't mind, now I think I'll rest."

"Certainly." I stand, Jocelyn doing the same beside me. "We'll be forever grateful to you for this story you've shared."

But her eyes are already closed.

After giving our goodbyes to Jane, we hurry toward the inn to get the others, our guards behind us. This has to be the answer.

A hidden room inside the library, and I'm going to find it.

Chapter
SEVENTEEN
❧

I T DOESN'T TAKE US long to get the others, tell them the story, and return to the library.

I hurry inside. The smell of smoke still permeates the air. I wonder how long the people here will have to deal with the aftereffects of such devastation.

The second thing I notice is how big it is in here. This place is vast, with shelves full of books everywhere. On the walls and in the middle of the floor. Rows and rows of them. The rows don't make sense at times, going perpendicular or being off center. Now that I know the design was meant to hide a secret room, it makes more sense.

"How are we ever going to find a secret room here?" I ask.

Next to me, Robert shakes his head.

"We'll find it," Jocelyn says.

"Doubtful," Reginald mutters. "There's too much in here. We couldn't find anything when we only had a few rows to go through."

He's right. We could spend years searching and never discover anything. I don't express my worries more than I already have. We've had enough upsetting times without my adding more to them. "I think we should start searching, then. Perhaps finding a secret room will be easier than spotting a single scroll." If the room is here.

"Let's get searching," Robert says.

Search we do. For two entire days, we look through the bookshelves, behind bookshelves, under books, behind scrolls, and anywhere else we can think of. On the third day, I'm ready to give up.

"There's nothing here," I say to Jocelyn. "Or if there is, it's so well hidden, we'll never find it."

"Don't give up hope yet," she says. "It could be around here somewhere."

"But every day we put it off is another day Robert and I aren't getting married."

"Maybe you should get married and then come back here to find the scrolls."

I sigh. "Probably. The problem is I'm afraid we'll not have time to return here for a while. We'll have duties to attend to. People to visit. Not to mention the fact that I'll want time to get to know Robert as my husband. Plus, I've been gone so much already, I'm not sure it would be wise to be gone even more."

"I could keep looking."

"You would?" Hope springs within me.

"It'd be a pleasure helping you out, especially since I know how much it means to you."

I give her a big hug. "Thank you. You really are the best friend I ever had."

She smiles. "Any time."

Andries peeks around one of the bookcases. "Any luck?"

"None," I say. "I don't think we're going to locate it this way."

"Me either, which is why I'm trying a different tactic. I measured the outside of the library. Now I'm going to measure the inside and check if there's a difference that doesn't account for the walls we see. If there is, it should give us an idea of where the hidden room is."

"Great idea." I follow him as he starts walking. It's then I realize he's pulling a string along with him that stretches back toward the front entrance. "Is this how you're measuring the building?" I ask.

"It is. Simple, but it should work."

Jocelyn and I follow him down rows of books against the outside wall. We come to a bookcase that's perpendicular to the wall.

"This makes things harder," Andries says.

Jocelyn hurries around it. From the other side, she yells, "Throw it through the bookcase."

He moves some books out of the way and shoves the string through.

"Got it," she says.

We hurry around to her and keep going. Robert joins us, and we tell him what we are doing.

"Sound plan," he says. "Here, let me help."

He grabs the string and hurries through the library until he reaches another bookcase perpendicular to the wall. We throw the string through again. We have to do so three more times before we get to the end of the building.

Robert holds the string still, while Andries looks at markings on it.

"It's the same size as the outside wall," he says. "There's nothing hidden. A least not here."

"Drat," Jocelyn says.

"Don't worry," Andries replies. "There are still three more walls to go and then we'll need to measure the middle of the room. Maybe even multiple spots."

The next wall proves to be further of a hassle than the first. More and more bookshelves cut our path, some even doubled or tripled up, pushing against each other. At one point, Robert has to climb up a bookshelf to retrieve the rope that got stuck.

When we come to the end, I find myself holding my breath as Andries looks the string over.

He shakes his head. "It's the same as the outside here too. I'm afraid this plan isn't going as I hoped it would."

"It's given us a way to see if it's along the outside walls," I say.

"It's more than we had before," Robert adds.

Perhaps we'll need a way to measure around these bookshelves too, but I can't imagine how to do that with so many of them. Or if the room is beneath us—how will we find it then? We'll have to move every bookshelf, which seems like an impossible feat, especially with books everywhere.

"Let's keep moving." Andries sounds as dejected as I feel.

I don't know that I want to go on. This is as useless as the search we were doing before. Nothing is coming up for all the work we've been putting forth. I push on anyway, trying to keep a grim expression from my face. I'm hot, tired, and hungry.

We repeat the process. Shelves are even more haphazard along this wall, some tilted at angles, creating little triangles of space. We search those openings, only to find regular old books.

We keep going until the far corner. At least we only have one last wall to measure. I wait for Andries to drag the string in so we can start the next one and be done with this useless project.

Only he doesn't.

"Here's something," he says. "The inside is shorter than the outside."

I look at the wall. Can it really be different? Can it be hiding a room that contains our history? Remembering the triangle bookshelves we found, I keep my excitement down. We've had a lot of disappointments. Still, it's hard not to think this might be it.

Andries takes several more measurements with Jocelyn's help while the rest of us stand around waiting. Though I want it to go faster, I say nothing. If he found it, it's worth my being patient.

Robert and I exchange a glance. He's hoping for the same thing as me, but it just as easily could be something else. Something wrong with the measurement. I go over to Robert, put my hand in his, and lean my head against him.

After several very long minutes, Andries looks up from his calculations with a grin. "It's here."

Chapter
EIGHTEEN
∾

"SEARCH THROUGH EVERYTHING," I say. "Take out all the books. Try to move the shelves. Whatever we can do to get through."

It doesn't take a moment for everyone to get moving. Jocelyn grabs books and makes careful stacks of them out of the way. Robert works on the shelves, but they won't budge.

"Let's concentrate on getting the books out," I say. "There's got to be something around here somewhere."

We're close. I can taste it. The feel of books in my hands, the way their scent fills the air, puts joy in my soul. Minus the smell of smoke that is. Even that doesn't deter me. That we may be close to finding what we've been searching for makes me more elated.

I shift through books and more books and even more books, until my arms ache. The elation has long since worn off when all the shelves are clear and there are stacks of books everywhere. I hope the librarian doesn't take this moment to come down the aisle. I can't imagine him being too happy about the mess we've made.

"I don't get it," Jocelyn says. "There's the extra space behind here. Why haven't we found a way to get in?"

"It must be well hidden," Andries says.

"Too well," I reply. That blacksmith knew what he was doing when he created this room.

I brush my hands along each shelf, hoping to find some latch or something that can move. Something that will let us in. The shelves are old and smooth from years of use. I run my palm across a flat surface, and my heart pounds when I find a latch in the back.

I flick my fingers along it, making it move. Nothing happens. Nothing at all. It's just a piece of wood. I run into three more like that. It's hard not to feel discouraged when we've come so close yet are so far away.

"Is there some magic you can use to find the entrance?" Jocelyn asks me.

I wipe my forehead with the back of my hand. "I'm not sure. There may be a way, but I don't know what it would be. Do you have any ideas, Andries?"

"Hm…Where do your specialties lie?"

"I can cast spells in nature and I can change my appearance."

The long lines of silence wait as he thinks. I do some thinking of my own. What can I do that would help us find our way through to the hidden room? I don't know for sure.

"What if you sent wisps of air around?" Andries asks. "See if there's anywhere the air can get through? Maybe that will have us finding a way to get in."

"That might just work."

The others give me space as I stand near the bookcases. I feel the air around me, let its stillness seep into me. I call on my magic, bringing it forward in a slow but steady stream. I pull the air around me. A whisper of a wind pulls up. I send it shooting all around this area of the library, focusing in on the walls we're trying to get through.

The breeze moves faster now, hurrying away from me, pulling my hair with it. I follow the air around with my magic, feeling through it. The books and walls are all hard, unrelenting sources that break the wind, splitting it off in an array of directions.

It spreads far over the walls, between the books and shelves. Some of the shelves it can go behind, but one it can't. I focus in on that wall, hoping to find a point that it can slip free through. Nothing. It's all broken against the walls and the shelf.

I try harder, hoping it's just lack of magic that's making it so I can't find a hole. Still, nothing. And then something. "I think I might have it. The air is moving through right here." I point to a section of the wall only to realize it's moving behind another shelf.

"You think it's back there?" Robert asks.

"I don't know. I thought I felt the air move back there, but now I'm thinking it was just going behind the bookcase."

"Let's move it anyway," Robert says. "Hurry to get the books off."

We rush forward, eager to see if there's anything behind the bookcase. We take book after book off, making neat stacks over to the side. It doesn't take long with all of us working to get the shelves cleared off. As soon as they're done, Andries and Robert go to move the shelf.

I clasp my hands together in front of me, hoping there's something there. As it moves away, my shoulders slump. Nothing but an aged wall. No hint of cracks or anything.

"I'm sorry," I say. "I must have felt it going behind the bookcase and mistaken that for something."

"It's not a total loss," Robert says, moving next to the wall perpendicular to the one he took the bookcase off of. "Look at this. The bookcase is part of the wall. It's been welded together into one piece."

I glace at it, and sure enough, there's nothing between the wall and the wood. It's all one piece. "You think the door is here somewhere?"

"That bookshelf certainly isn't going anywhere."

All at once, we rummage through the bookshelf, getting dirty from the dust flying from the shelves. I don't even care if we can find it. But when we come up for air, there's still no sign of an entrance.

"Can we break our way in through the bookcase and wall?" Robert asks.

"We could try," Andries says, "but there's no guarantee we'll be able to make it in without the door. What's more important, we could unknowingly damage the scrolls we're looking for. It'd be a high price to pay for getting in."

"So you're saying we need patience?" Jocelyn says. "I'm no good at that."

"Me neither." I want to sit on the floor and fall asleep. Too bad it isn't only dirty but littered with books. "Perhaps we should call it a day." Though it's mid afternoon, I'm ready to be done. "We can have the librarians keep a look out so no one else gets in here. I'm stumped."

Robert puts an arm around me. My body tingles, his presence rejuvenating me. "It will be all right. We're so close. We'll find it," he says.

I hope no one blows it up in the meantime. I don't dare say that out loud, though I wonder if the others are thinking it. It's a dangerous time we're living in. Perhaps we shouldn't tell the librarian. What if he was the one who blew up part of the library in the first place? Sure, he seemed upset, but anyone could be behind this.

I shake the thoughts from my head. It was more likely the pirates, anyway. I need sleep. "We should go."

"It's a good idea to take a break," Robert says. He moves to my side, brushing one of the shelves of the bookcase like he isn't ready to go yet.

"A break?" Andries asks, like he's never heard of such a thing. He probably hasn't. The man works himself to pieces. I guess it's what happened when he didn't have Constance anymore; he threw himself into his work.

Jocelyn heads toward the exit. At least, I think she does; it's hard to tell the way out in such a maze. I grab a hold of the shelf next to the one Robert touches and try to pull it out. I feel like throwing something. Of course it doesn't move. I shift it, trying to loosen it. Suddenly, the bookcase next to me swings open, hitting Robert.

"Ow," he says.

"I think this is it," I say. Energy courses back through me. "I think we've found the secret room."

Jocelyn comes running back. Robert opens the door wider, and Andries peers in. We all do.

It's dark in here. All I can make out are cobwebs.

"I'm getting torches." Robert hurries off before we can reply.

While he's gone, I think about going in, but the cobwebs scare me off. I still remember the baby spiders that infested the last cave I was in.

Robert doesn't take long to return. It must not be a very big room. He gives us each a torch, lighting them with his own already lit torch as he does so. When we all have lit torches, he holds his up to the secret room.

The room is a dark gray, even with the light he shines in. It's made out of some type of large stone. It's bigger than I thought it would be, taking up more space than it would appear from the outside.

"Do you think there's magic making this room bigger than the space?" I ask.

"Most definitely," Andries replies.

There's a table in the center with scrolls and a statue of a gargoyle on it. More shelves with scrolls line the walls. There must be a plethora of information in here. I wonder why these scrolls were cut off from the rest of the library? Is it just because they are the oldest, or is there something else more at play here?

I step forward. "What we're looking for has to be in here somewhere."

"Be careful," Andries says. "I don't know how well the scrolls have held up without looking them over."

The dusty room reminds me of the cave we found that was also covered in a layer of grime, though not as much as I'd expect from a room that hasn't been cleaned in who knows how long.

We need to find the right place where the scrolls were put. The problem is this place is much larger than the cave was. It's going to be a lot harder to find anything in here.

"Robert, Jocelyn, and I will take the far end. Reginald and Andries, why don't you start here? We can meet in the middle, and if we still haven't found something, we can switch sides to make sure we cover everything."

"Sounds like a good plan to me," Andries says.

Reginald looks at Robert with undisguised longing. The guy is creepy. Why is he so obsessed with humans?

It's rather mucky work searching through the area. The gray cast gives the room a grim feel. I hope we can find what I need. It's rather well organized, but nothing is labeled and with so many scrolls, there's bound to be lots of wrong choices before we get to the right one.

I'm careful to keep my torch away from the scrolls as I search through them with gloved hands. None of this is particularly useful. More of the same we found before, only these go back much further than the previous scrolls we looked at. The age gives me hope.

We continue like that for what seems like hours. Nothing looks like a possibility. Nothing at all. I worry the part of history I seek is lost for good. That somehow, wherever it was, it got destroyed. Or maybe it wasn't even here to begin with.

"I think I found something," Robert calls out.

I rush to his side, where he has a vase open and is looking inside it.

Robert puts his hand in the vase and pulls out a scroll. My breathing comes in fast. What if this is it? What if we've found the scroll we've been looking for? What is it going to tell us? Will it be some help to our countries, like we hope it will be? Our history could very well be in Robert's gloved hands right now. Literally.

Robert gives the scroll to Andries, who's shaking. Andries moves to the closest table and wipes it off with a handkerchief. Once the area is cleared, he carefully puts the scroll down and very gently begins unrolling it.

I watch the process, holding my torch high, so we can all see what it is Robert found.

The scroll is dotted with age. It's hard to read through everything, and the familiar script isn't the easiest to decipher. What is legible reads:

> *Difficult times have overrun the land. No one can escape them. We elves were once great friends of humans, but now I fear that time has passed. Our two races always knew harmony, until greed and selfishness took hold of two hearts.*

"I think this is it," Andries says. "I really do. I need to get it back to Amara, so I can work with it properly."

"Can you make out any more of it?" I ask.

"No, I can't," Andries says. "But I can clean it up. And this looks to be in the same hand as the other two scrolls, so I'm certain this is it."

"Should we look for other scrolls?" Robert asks.

"Perhaps," I say. "But not now. We've got the one we came for. We'll send someone qualified to look through these all. Who knows what they may contain."

But we found it. The one we need. Against all odds, we now have more of the common history of our two races. Of the prophecy that said I, or some elven princess, need to marry a human prince to unite our two countries. I am that princess. Robert is that human.

The one prophecy about to come true.

Chapter
NINETEEN

❧

"WE FOUND IT," I tell Mother as soon as we return to the inn. "I can't wait to get it back to Amara and find out what it says."

"You certainly have taken up quite the interest in history lately. I'm glad this worked out for you." Mother stands from her chair and walks over to me. "Does this mean it's time to go home?"

"It does. I'm anxious to get there and start preparing for the wedding."

"And there's nothing I'd like more than to help you." She takes me by both shoulders, though I'm an inch taller than her. Yet, she still doesn't look me in the eye as she says, "My, how you've grown. It seems like just the other day you were a wee thing, and here we are, getting ready to marry you off." She lets go. "I'll make sure all arrangements are taken care of. We want to get going as soon as possible."

Before she leaves the room, I say, "What do you think of Robert?"

"What do I think of him?" She pauses. "I think he's very gentlemanly. He sure seems to care for you a lot. I haven't seen his level of attention to a loved one in a long, long time."

My instinct is to ask about her relationship with my father, but I'm not sure I want to know. They've always been kind to one another, but it doesn't seem to go beyond a friendly affection.

Still, maybe this is the best time to ask even if it's hard to hear. "What about you and father?"

"What about us?"

"Do the two of you love each other, or have you ever loved each other?"

She grows quiet. It's not the usual silence emanating from her, but a deeper one. One that reaches my core. When she speaks, it's with a voice I don't understand. A depth of feeling I've not at any time heard from her. "Your father is a good man, and I appreciate him for it, but I've never loved him like you seem to love Robert."

Feeling brave, I continue asking questions. "Do you ever wish it was different?"

"Oh, child. When you get to be my age, you realize there are more important things than love. Like our country, for example. I have to do what is best for our people."

"I understand that." But I don't have to like it. While I want to do what's best for my country, I feel blessed to have found true love with Robert, and I hope it continues to grow and helps me become a better person.

"Are you getting nervous about the wedding?" Mother asks.

I shake my head, a big grin stealing over my face. "I've never been so excited for something in my life. It's going to be the best day."

Mother doesn't move; she only looks at me, though not at my face.

"I love him, Mother. I really do love him. I didn't think that could ever happen. I was determined to be happy with the man you and Father chose for me, but I didn't expect to fall in love. But I do love him. I can't wait to spend the rest of my life with him."

"Well"—she pulls herself up straighter—"I'd best see to the preparations."

Happiness trills through me. "I'll tell the others we're leaving as soon as possible."

I'm the luckiest elf in the world. I found my piece of history. Hopefully, it will tell us more soon. I've got the man I love, and I have a good family. Everything is looking up.

Chapter
TWENTY

THE DAY IS AS RAINY as I've ever seen. We've been on the road for three days, and each day keeps getting worse. Before the rain, we could see for miles around us. There's nothing in this area to block our view of the landscape, but with the rain coming down in sheets, it's hard to see anything.

"I wonder if this is a consequence to someone's spell," I say. I still wish I was in a carriage with Jocelyn instead of Reginald, but it is what it is. "I haven't seen weather this bad since my own spell when I was on the pirate ship." Getting ready to marry Octavian. I shudder.

"It could be," Robert says. "Or it could just be a very bad rain. We get rain like this sometimes in Bardus."

Suddenly the carriage goes faster.

"This is a dangerous speed in this weather," I say.

Robert moves to the window—I guess to tell them to slow down. Instead, he yells back at us, "Get down."

Not knowing why, I duck as much as I can in this infernal dress. If I wasn't traveling with Mother, I would have something more practical on. This is one more case for the clothes I like. "What is it?"

Robert leans away from the window, pulling out his sword. "Pirates."

Reginald leans closer to the window and says with glee, "Pirates."

"Get back, you fool," Robert says.

I groan. Not again. I'm sick of pirates. "What if they got a hold of another elf to control the weather?"

"It's possible," Robert says. "Can you do anything about it?"

"How close are they?"

"Still a ways out but getting closer."

"I'll try." I pull all my magic toward me, calling it together.

"Don't overextend yourself, Arabella," Mother says.

I want to tell her to stop distracting me and use her own magic, but I realize I don't even know what type of magic she has. Instead, I focus on the task at hand. I tell my magic to clear the rain away. A big feat, if it's a normal storm, but I think I can do it. I release my magic, and the carriage sloshes down the road.

The pull on my magic is tough. "This isn't a natural downpour."

Robert puts a hand on my shoulder, but as quickly as it's there, it's gone, and he's back looking out the window. "The guards are gathering around us. It's going to be a tough fight, though."

The magic that created this storm is strong. I'm fighting against it, working to bend it to my will. Sweat breaks out on my forehead. I ignore it and push more magic out into the sky. This has to stop.

The water in the clouds moves against my magic, making me feel like I'm in a damp cloud. But there's something else there. Something like the brush of a finger—only a magical one. I shove at it as hard as I can.

It bends against my force, moving away as I think of the clouds keeping their water. The rain outside slows.

With a sudden push, the magical finger turns into a hand that chokes my magic. The rain pounds harder than ever. I have to overcome whoever is up there.

I send all my magic, every drop of it, straight at the hand. It doesn't budge. "I can't get through," I say.

"Don't strain yourself, darling." Mother's voice is panicked. "I can't have you hurt. The guards will protect us from the pirates."

"Can you think of a way around it?" Robert asks.

I close my eyes and let my magic settle back against the abrasive other magic. What can I do? How can I get around this? *That's it.* Around the magic, instead of through it. I concentrate on my magic again. Push hard against the other. As soon as it starts to push back, I jump my magic backward and dart around my opponent. I slip past, cutting off their supply of magic.

The rain stops.

"Got it," I say.

"Just in time," Robert says. "They're getting close."

My head starts to spin. "Oh, no. I'm getting dizzy. I hope that's not a consequence of the spell."

"Not my little girl," Mother says.

"You have to fight it," Robert says. "If the guards fail, I'll need you to back me up. I trust you. You can do this."

"Right. Just give me a minute."

"You don't have a minute," Reginald says. "They're here."

"The guards are staying by our side," Robert says.

I rest my head against the coach, as the sound of swords clashing reaches me. The carriage slows.

"Stop right now," a male voice calls out.

"Go faster," Robert calls out the window.

But the carriage stops. There's a *thunk*, and then the pirates are upon us. I push past my dizziness and pull out my sword. A pirate sticks his head in the window, and I slash at him. He darts back.

"Arabella," Robert calls out. "Are you all right?"

"I'll be fine," I say, thrusting my sword toward a second opponent. "You protect yourself and my mother."

"What about me?" Reginald says. "These humans won't care how much I like them."

Finally he gets it. Why did we have to bring such a bumbling fool with us? There's not time to think about it as the door on Robert's side is ripped open. The pirates have left my side. They're after him.

Even with the guards fighting, it's not looking good. I jump out of my carriage, ignoring Mother calling for me to come back, and hurry to the other side of the carriage. A fresh wave of dizziness hits me, as I round the corner. The world sways before me as a dozen or so pirates and a few elves make way for Captain Smythe.

"Fancy meeting you again," he says.

I force myself to ignore the woozy feeling that wants to take me down. I can't give in now. "This time will be the last."

"We can both agree on that."

"Leave her alone," Robert calls, hopping out of the carriage.

"Oh, I plan on it." Captain Smythe heads straight for Robert, his massive frame making for a fearsome opponent.

Robert brings up his sword, but Captain Smythe's bulk hides anything that happens after that.

A pirate comes at me, swinging his sword wildly, like he's not trying to fight me but distract me. I can't let him. I try to sidestep him, but he sticks his sword out so I can't. I block him. There's no way I can go around him without fighting him, but there's no time to fight him.

The mud squishes beneath my feet as I thrust my sword forward. I slip. Fall. Covered in mud, I use the opportunity to slash at my opponent from underneath. He falls back with a cry, and I get back on my feet. Captain Smythe is fighting Robert with unmatched ferocity. More pirates come toward me, but there's no chance to take them all out.

I call on my magic as I hurry toward Captain Smythe. I pull at the clouds, searching for what I need. It's not there. How am I going to stop the men behind me? How do I plan on taking on Captain Smythe?

Everything seems hopeless. After all we've been through, all we've done, this is what it comes down to. Losing the man I love to Captain Smythe right before my very eyes. I hope they don't attack my mother next because there's nothing I'd be able to do to stop them. I can't even protect Robert.

I feel what I was looking for. A spark. As I haste onward, I use my magic to make it grow and stretch. I've got it. I bring it down behind me in a giant bolt of lightning.

There's a flash of light and a *crack*. I can feel the energy trailing after me, but I don't stop. Don't do anything except run to Robert, who is weakening against Captain Smythe. I have to get to him on time.

Robert swings upward, but Captain Smythe dashes him down. Robert's movements are getting slower as he lunges backward. Captain Smythe advances on him until he's back at the carriage. He's caught.

I come from behind. As I'm about to slash at Captain Smythe with my sword, someone behind me yells, "Captain, watch out."

Captain Smythe whirls around, parrying my blade as I'm thrusting it toward him. He forces my blade aside. I twirl it around his sword and come back to him. The fight grows more intense.

Robert stumbles toward us. I see what he's doing. If we work together, we may make it. I keep Captain Smythe distracted as long as I can, waving my sword around. He hits my blade so hard, it almost jumps from my hand. I keep my grip and thrust it toward his abdomen. He blocks, as Robert hits him on the head.

Captain Smythe falls to the ground, and I kick his sword away from him, putting my blade to his throat. Robert's sword joins mine. The guards are all still engaged with the pirates around them, outnumbered, but with Captain Smythe down, it looks as some of those pirates are ready to run away.

I stand over Captain Smythe, heart pounding in triumph. "You are scum. You will never again see the light of day if I have anything to do with it."

"There's something you should know," Captain Smythe says.

"I know everything I need to—thank you very much."

He has the gall to smile at me. *Smile.* "Suit yourself."

Infuriating man. No matter. I finally have him on the right end of my sword.

Chapter
TWENTY-ONE

I T TAKES A WHILE to get all our guards to come to, but with Captain Smythe tied up, his goonies run off. I should probably be more worried about them, but frankly, I feel he is the instigator of all the problems we have, even if elves were involved.

His attack proves humans and elves can work together.

Once Captain Smythe is taken care of, what other enemy do we have? Nothing. A few skirmishes maybe, but they'll be easily squelched. No one has the commanding power he does—or rather, did.

Mother is frantic over my fighting but doesn't leave the carriage. She keeps saying things like "Come back to the carriage, Arabella" and "It's not safe." Even after all the pirates are gone, she's still worrying after me.

Our guards are rounded up and patched up the best we can. Not that there's much we can do out here, but thankfully, none of their injuries are serious. There are cuts and bruises all around, but it could be worse. It's a testament to our guards' skill that they weren't slaughtered by that blood-thirsty bunch.

The other carriage nears and stops.

"Is the fighting over?" the driver calls out.

"It is," I call back.

"Is everyone all right?" Jocelyn asks from the carriage window.

"I think so." Joy pulses through me. "We caught Captain Smythe."

She gasps.

"I think it's time we got him back to my father so he can have his punishment doled out," I say.

Robert leans against the carriage, looking far too pale. "That would be wise."

I spoke too soon to Jocelyn. I rush to him. "Are you all right?"

He shakes his head. "I feel a little faint, truth be told."

"I'm not surprised after you took on Captain Smythe," I say.

He puts a hand on his stomach. "I think it's something more. I didn't notice until the adrenaline wore off."

"What is it?" I ask, more concerned than ever before. It's then I notice his shirt has been ripped. I pull his coat away to expose dark red oozing from him.

He slumps against the carriage.

"Robert!"

Chapter
TWENTY-TWO
◞

WE GET ROBERT in the carriage while a guard goes ahead on horseback to find the nearest healer. I hold a cloth to Robert's wound, hoping to stem the flow of blood. I call on my magic, but I fear it's not enough. I don't have the knowledge or skill to heal a wound like this. Still, I have to try.

I send my magic down in a vast wave, carrying my health to his. If only I knew how to deal with the wound itself.

The drive lasts forever, our carriage bumping and swaying. I keep pouring my health magic into him, but it doesn't do much good. He grows paler by the moment.

"Take some of my health," Jocelyn says. She's alone with me in my carriage—Reginald, Mother, and her lady's maid following in the other carriage, along with Captain Smythe who's been tied up and lashed to the top of the carriage like baggage. It was a feat getting him up there, and kind of mean, but we all thought it was most fitting and the safest thing to do with him.

I can't think of the pirate now, if I want to keep my head.

Normally, I'd hesitate at an offer such as Jocelyn's, but not today. I grab her hand and call on all the health she can spare, and send it to Robert. Through my magic, I can tell it helps make him stronger, but it doesn't stop the bleeding.

Will the ride never end? Will we never find a healer? I'm losing Robert for real this time and with my hands still on him. Blood seeps between my fingers as I try to put pressure on the wound. There's nothing more I can do. I don't know how to stop this.

"Hold on," I whisper in his ear. "Just hold on."

Still, the journey continues. I continue whispering words of encouragement to him. That's all there is left that I know how to do. There's no more health I or Jocelyn can spare without passing out ourselves, and we'd be less use to him if we were unconscious.

"I don't know what to do," I say to Jocelyn. Tears run down my face.

She puts a hand on my shoulder. "We'll be there soon. I know it."

"But what if it's too late? He's lost so much blood."

"You've given him all the health we can spare. I'm sure it's buoyed him."

"Maybe, but it doesn't feel like enough."

By the time we stop, my hands are crimson with his blood. He's pale. Oh, so pale.

"He'll make it," Jocelyn says.

For once, I don't believe her.

Chapter
TWENTY-THREE

I'M WEAK AFTER the ordeal of trying to heal Robert. There's still no word on whether or not he'll survive. The worst part is I'm stuck in bed, recovering from giving him so much of my health.

"He'll be all right," Jocelyn says from the bed next to mine. She knows me well enough to understand my worries.

"I don't know. There was so much blood."

"But we got him here before he bled all the way out. They'll know how to help him."

"What if they don't?"

She reaches across the space between our beds and grabs my hand. "You're so strong. Stronger than you know. You can handle whatever comes." Her grip is weak, despite the reassurance in her words.

"I'm sorry I had to take so much health from you to heal him," I say.

"Don't be. I was happy to give it. He is my future king, after all."

I sigh. What will happen if he dies? Not just to me, but to all of Bardus? I don't know if they can handle another heir to the throne dying. Maybe Princess Belle would take back her abdication.

I don't want to be thinking this way, but I can't help myself.

"Jocelyn, I'm going to ask you something, but you don't have to answer if it hurts too much to talk about."

"What is it?"

"How did you handle it when Abner died?" I know it's not the same as what Robert and I have gone through, but it still seems like she'd have better insight than me.

She's silent for so long, I think she's not going to answer. I curse myself for asking in the first place. I shouldn't bring up her pain. I'm sure it still hurts.

"It was hard," she says, in a pained way that rips at my heart. "We were only just beginning to know each other on a deeper level while you were gone up Mount Incidium. That time was so dear. I had feelings for him before, but that was when I really started to fall in love with him.

"I disliked him at first. He was so mean to you. But then he was nicer. I didn't know how to feel when I found out he was the one who told you Robert was dead. It was a cruel lie to tell, and I didn't want to love anyone that was cruel. But my feelings were still there, just tainted.

"As I came to realize he was genuinely sorry for what he put you through, I was able to forgive him for it. And from there, my feelings for him continued to grow, though like I told you before, it was always hard knowing you were supposed to marry him. It just didn't seem right."

"I would much rather that you had been able to marry him instead of what took place."

The silence is interrupted only by the pangs in my heart.

"Did you know that Princess Belle used to put frogs in his bed?" she asks.

I laugh. "What?"

"Frogs terrified him. He found them to be slimy and gross when he was a boy. The sound they made only confirmed his dislike for them. He thought for sure they would do something bad to him. So whenever he and his sister got in a fight, she'd hide a frog or two in his bed."

"I had no clue she could be like that. I'll have to ask her about it next time I see her."

"Definitely do," Jocelyn says. "I'm certain she has more stories that would surprise us both. And that's what I got while you were gone—a softer side of Abner. One neither you nor I saw before. He was so… real. I didn't know a prince could be like that."

"Honestly, I didn't either. I thought he was too sour to have any redeeming qualities."

"I think he listened to too many rumors about elves and their magic. That's why he was the way he was when we first met him. The person underneath that exterior was kind and funny."

She hasn't really answered my question, but talking about it seems to have done her good. Her voice is lighter. Happier. She truly did love him.

"I wish he was still here." A wistful note enters her tone. "Although you'd have to marry him, and a relationship between me and him could never be."

"Things should have been different. Marriage between the two of you could have taken place. This politics stuff shouldn't get in the way of love and happiness."

"But it does."

"It does."

We're both silent for some time. My mind wanders back to Robert and how he's doing. It's stressful to think of what he's been through. What he's going through now. What might happen to him. It makes me want to rush out of this bed, to go find him, but I haven't the energy.

"I didn't handle Abner's death well," Jocelyn says. "I've felt lost since it happened. I don't know what to do with myself. I don't know what to do without him. He's gone. Killed before my eyes."

"I'm sorry."

She sniffs. "Me too. I keep hoping I'll feel better about everything soon, and I have a little bit, but it still doesn't make things all right," she says. "But I'm sure you won't have that problem with Robert. You gave him so much health, he has no choice but to survive."

I'd like to think she's right, but I don't know. "I'm ready to contemplate something else. Something distracting."

"What about the wedding? Are you ready for it?" she asks.

"We'll see what Mother has planned. I don't know what she's thought of this time. As long as it's not as fancy as the last one."

"You looked beautiful, though."

"But it wasn't really me."

"That's true."

"You two are supposed to be resting," a healer says as she comes in the room.

"How is Robert?" I ask, ignoring her admonishing.

"It's too soon to tell," is the only reply I get.

"I need more than that. You can't leave me hanging."

"Our best healer is with him. We're doing everything we can."

By the look in her eye, everything they can do may not be enough.

Chapter
TWENTY-FOUR

⁓

I WALK IN THE ROOM, scared of what's in here. I know what they've said, but it doesn't make this easier. Robert is white and unmoving as I approach him. My heart is low, far past the ground beneath my feet.

I kneel at his side and place a hand on his chest. Fear and pain jolts through me. I don't know how Jocelyn survived losing someone she loved. The situations are so different and yet so similar.

I put my head on his shoulder and cry. A hand pats my head.

Robert. My Robert.

"Please, no tears," he says. "I'm fine now. I promise."

"But you're still so sick. What if you get an infection? What if you lost too much blood?"

"Don't worry about me. Everything is going to be all right. You elves have amazing medical skills. We humans have a lot to learn from you. We should get some elves over on Bardus, to help do magic on our patients."

"You shouldn't be thinking of these things at a time like this."

"I'm the future king. I have to think about things like this at all times."

I sniff. "I know, but you gave me a heart attack. I thought you were going to die."

"But I didn't. Everything is fine now. I'm safe, and as soon as I get better, we're getting married."

For the first time since I entered the room, I smile. "We are."

"And this time Captain Smythe won't be there to stop the wedding."

"No one will stop us." I grin, my heart lifting.

Though he's still recovering, he smiles back, putting a hand on my cheek.

"Jocelyn said you would get better," I say.

"Wise woman. You should try listening to her."

"I would if it wasn't so darn hard to do," I say teasingly, and then grow serious. "It's so difficult. I've lost Constance. I can't imagine losing you too."

"You don't have to. I'm right here."

Chapter
TWENTY-FIVE
◡

W E'RE IN THE CARRIAGE again. I worry over Robert every time we jostle or hit a bump, which seems to be constantly. I'll be happy when this journey is over. Happier when he's fully recovered.

"Are you doing all right?" I ask him.

"As good as can be expected." He holds back a grimace.

"I'm sorry you're hurting."

"Don't be. You saved my life. Besides," he says, "we finally defeated Captain Smythe. That alone is reason to celebrate."

"It is, isn't it?" I grin, wide and happy. "We need to have a party, I think. When you're feeling better, of course."

"Why wait?"

"Because we don't want you to reinjure yourself."

"I just hope we don't have to push back the wedding far."

"Oh, don't say that. Of course I want you healthy for the wedding, but I don't know how much longer I can wait."

He smiles and tips in closer. "I can't wait, either."

I giggle, a giddy feeling spreading through my core. There's never been a happier time in my life. Robert's lips look oh-so kissable. I want to lean right in and feel them against mine. Feel how soft they are.

I'm actually angling forward. Not how I pictured my first kiss—in the bumpy seat of a carriage while Robert is injured—but I'll take it. He seems to read it in my eyes and lowers his head. A thrill rushes through me.

Mother stirs. I back away from Robert but take his hand. If she wakes, she'll have to deal with us holding hands. We are to be married, after all. But I'll wait on that kiss until a better time. I'm eager for it, I want to feel his lips on mine, but I don't want it to be while my mother watches. Besides, it would shock her beyond all reason.

"When do you think you'll be feeling up for the wedding?" I ask Robert.

"The healer said a month until I'm more myself again, but I don't want to wait that long."

"We're going to need longer than that to plan," Mother says.

"Will we really?" I ask. "We've waited so long. I think the people need to see us unite as soon as possible."

"The people need to see you get married in a proper way," she says.

Reginald chooses that moment to speak up. I thought he was sleeping. "The queen is right. The people need to see a proper wedding."

Embarrassment fills me that he caught Robert and me being so gushy together, but there's nothing we can do about it now. "But why wait?" I ask. "We've been through this. The arrangements should already be made for the most part. We'll only need a few tweaks here and there."

"But darling," Mother says, "we can't use things from your last wedding. Not only would it be tacky, but some things can't be reused—like your ruined wedding gown."

Right. The gown. Mother was not happy when she found it was muddied and torn and left with Teresa, Robert's mother. What was I supposed to do? Take it with me while on the run? Teresa promised to send all the diamonds decorating it back to us, which I trust her to do. But honestly, I don't want another diamond-heavy gown. Something simple would suit me much better. How do I get my mother to understand that?

"You're right," I say. "We can't reuse the gown. I'd be happy to help design a new one. It'll be much more to my liking, and something that could be made in a matter of"—hours—"weeks. I'm certain the rest of the arrangements can be made quickly as well."

Mother sniffs. "Well, we can consider moving it up. But there's no guarantee. We need to make sure this is an event people won't forget."

"It's true," I say, feeling brave against my mother. She may be the queen, but this is my wedding. And they are my people as well. I have to do what I think is best for them. "But it's also an event we need, to unite our two races. I think we should consider having it on Sulamay Island. Though it technically belongs to the elves, it's more of a middle ground. It would make it easier for more humans to attend than last time."

"But Sulamay Island is so run down."

"We can fix up what we need to. Between hard work and magic, I'm certain we can do it."

"In years, maybe."

"If I can arrange to have it done sooner, will you allow us to be married in the near future?"

"Fine. I suppose. If you can fix things up quickly, we can have the wedding sooner than I hoped for."

I give Robert's hand a squeeze. With this type of motivation, this will be the fastest renovation ever.

Chapter
TWENTY-SIX

W HEN WE ARRIVE in Amara, the first thing I
do is have a healer look over Robert.

"He is fine. Everything will heal as it should,"
the woman says to me, easing my concerns. She turns to
Robert. "You should still sit back for a while. No more sword
fights."

"I'd be all for that," he replies.

"I mean it, now. Take it easy."

"I'll make sure he does," I say.

Robert gives me a grin. "Not even married yet, and you're
already taking care of me."

"I do what I can." I'm happy he's fine and nothing else is
going to happen to him. He's safe and healthy.

After that visit, we head straight to the throne room, where
my father is waiting. We tell him everything that happened
while we were gone, focusing on the fact that we captured
Captain Smythe.

"I can't believe you finally caught the elusive pirate," Father says. "Tell me again how you did it?"

"Don't encourage her," Mother says.

"She did an excellent job," Robert says, surprising me by going against my mother. "While I hope she doesn't ever have to face circumstances like that again, she handled it well."

"I've kept my mouth shut because you were injured, but I can't anymore. She could have been hurt because of you," Mother tells Robert. "If you hadn't pushed her, she wouldn't have been so worn out. Think what it would have done to her magic if she hadn't won."

"He was hurt," I say. "He could have died. He almost did."

"But he didn't. And you almost died too."

"Mother, I'm fine. Really. Please don't worry about me so much."

"I'm a mother. It's what I do."

"That's enough," my father says. "I agree that you shouldn't put yourself in danger, Arabella, but I'm proud of how you handled yourself."

"Thank you."

"I can't believe how grown up my littler girl is." He wraps me in a hug. These are becoming happily common in my life. "I've placed Captain Smythe in prison for now. We'll have a trial to decide his fate, but I can't imagine it will be a good one."

I shudder, grateful I don't have to witness death sentences being carried out. "As long as he can't hurt anyone ever again."

"He's got a dozen guards watching over him in our most impenetrable dungeon cell, besides the usual precautions. He won't be getting out," Father says. "Now, about this wedding business… Are you certain you want to have it on Sulamay Island? It will probably take longer to get everything set up than you're hoping for."

"I think it will be a good show for the people, both ours and the humans."

"Very well. You'd best get to work, then."

Getting to work is something I can do. We hurry from the room.

Once we're out of earshot of my mother, I slow down. "You shouldn't hassle my mother like that," I say to Robert.

"I'm sorry. It's only that I know how hard you worked. I wasn't trying to put you in danger or encourage it, but you have a lot of raw talent that needs to be recognized."

"Thank you." The fact he's willing to say so and believes it means a lot to me. "I want you to have a good relationship with my family."

"I understand completely. I want you to have a good relationship with mine as well."

We understand each other, even if things are hard sometimes. I take his hand. "Now, to prepare for our wedding."

He grins. "I'll invite all the humans I know who can help fix up the castle and surrounding area."

"And I'll invite all the elves I know."

"Soon enough, we'll be getting married."

Not only that, but it will be a good test of how well our races can get along. I hope it goes more smoothly than I'm expecting.

Chapter
TWENTY-SEVEN
‿

SULAMAY ISLAND is as I recall it. The dock is rotting, and the castle is falling apart. Literally. The stones are coming off or crumbling. It's going to take more work than I told Mother it would.

"Perhaps this wasn't such a good idea," I say.

"What are you talking about?" Robert says. "This will be perfect. Once we get the place cleaned up a little, that is."

"Maybe, but I'm afraid it's going to take a lot of time."

"You're that anxious to be married to me, huh?"

I wrap my arms around him. "As a matter of fact, I am."

"Sorry to interrupt," Jocelyn says, "but there's a boatload of people waiting behind you to get to work."

We pull apart, my cheeks heating. "Of course. We want them to get to cleaning this place up, after all."

It doesn't take long to get everyone working together. It's mostly elves doing the labor. They and the few humans here keep their distance as much as possible, but they still come together as they need to.

An occasional argument breaks out but dies the instant Robert or I show up. It's like they want to work together in peace but can't quite seem to. I hope, with time, the disagreements will turn to friendship.

The week passes slowly. The amount of work getting done isn't nearly what I want it to be. Maybe my mother was right and this was a bad location to choose to be married. Bad location. Bad mix of humans and elves trying to fix it.

"How are we ever going to finish this?" I ask Robert.

"More people will come, and things will go faster."

"They'll have to go a lot faster. The pace is crawling right now."

"Hey, now." He puts an arm around my shoulders. "Don't be too down on yourself. They're getting a lot accomplished, and we've got several more boatloads of people coming."

"But won't more humans and elves mean more arguing?"

"They'll come to work together. I know they can."

"You're right. I guess I'm anxious to be married."

He pulls me closer. "So am I."

I'm breathless. Being around him has that effect on me. I want to lean in and never let go.

"New boat just came in," Layla, an elf helping us out, says.

"Thank you." Robert doesn't take his eyes from mine.

"We have to go greet the people like good rulers should." Not that we're rulers yet, but rulers-in-training should as well. If we're to lead these people someday, we have to do our best now.

"Let's go, then," Robert says, but before I move, he pulls me into a hug that's warm and sure.

Everything is going to be all right, no matter how tough things seem.

We stroll down to the boat together. A crewman ties the ship on the brand new dock. The old one was so dilapidated that it was the first thing we fixed upon arrival. Now it is fit for the slew of people that will be coming to help and for the wedding itself. Its freshly made boards are strong and running so long that four or five boats can fit alongside it. Not many compared to Amara's port, but more than the one that could fit here before.

The crew sets up the gangplank so it's sturdy against the dock. The first person off the boat is Emeline. My surprise leaves me speechless.

"Emeline," Robert says, and I can't read the tone of his voice.

She gives us both a curtsey.

"What are you doing here?" I ask her, not hiding my shock at seeing her.

"I've come to help." She gives me a shy smile. "The king gave me permission to work here for the wedding."

I'm not sure how I feel about this. I did forgive her, but it's still hard to move on. "Thank you for coming," I say. "We could use all the help we can get if we're to be ready on time."

"I was hoping you'd say that," she says.

I give her what I hope is an encouraging smile. "Layla will show you to your room and where we need help." I motion to Layla.

"Thank you so much. I can't tell you how much I'm excited to be here."

There's no time to think about Emeline any more. More elves come off the ship, one by one but quickly. I greet them all, happy for their warm replies. The last elves head off to the castle to find their room, and I'm about to follow them when more people disembark. Humans.

If I knew humans were on board, I would have had them get off the ship together with the elves instead of being held back to last.

"Do you think we'll ever see the day when they'll come down together?" I ask Robert.

"I don't know for certain, but I hope."

Hope. It's the only thing we have.

I greet the humans alongside Robert. Most are cautious around me but friendly enough. A few are standoffish, and even less are downright rude. What are they doing here if they don't like me in the first place? I'm going to have to keep more than my sword with me. I'm going to need guards on my own island.

As soon as the last of the humans is gone, Robert suggests that very thing.

Except I won't put up with it. "I can't have your people more scared of me than they already are. I'm afraid if I walk around with a pack of guards surrounding me, it will alienate them more."

"What about Stewart? He looks more like a nice grandpa than a guard."

I laugh. "Don't let him hear you call him that."

"I'll keep that in mind. But really, he looks safe, yet he's lethal. I think he'd be a good choice."

"Fine. If he doesn't mind hanging out with me, I can handle having him around."

More than that, I'd enjoy his company, even if it's not for the reason I'd like.

Chapter
TWENTY-EIGHT
☙

FOUR DAYS LATER, another boat arrives with Andries in tow. I rush out to greet him, Stewart close by like he's been since Robert and I talked. Andries hurries down the ramp. We're both anxious to see each other, which I hope means he found something.

"What news do you have for us?" I ask after a warm greeting.

"The scroll has been cleaned and made readable. I've got a copy of it here with me. The original is with the other two scrolls in Amara."

"What does it say?"

"I think we'd better go get Robert for this."

"Of course." Though I'm a little surprised he won't open up and tell me what it says, I'm more than happy to have Robert at my side as I read it.

We hurry through the construction of the castle until we find Robert working on repairing the rotted out floor of a room.

Robert stands and moves toward us the moment he spots me. They exchange pleasantries, and then he asks, "Is there news?"

"Yes," Andries replies. "I've uncovered what the scroll says."

"Let's see what's on it," he says.

We hurry down the hall and stairs, through yet another hall, to an area of the castle that's not being worked on—the kitchen. It's empty for the moment. It wouldn't be if Constance was still alive. The thought brings a pang to my chest. I wonder how she'd react to having both the copy of the scroll and Andries here. I'll never know now.

Andries pulls out the scroll and places it on the table, pulling my thoughts away from the elf I miss more than words can say.

I glance down at the scroll. It reads:

> *Difficult times have overrun the land. No one can escape them. We elves were once great friends of the humans, but now I fear that time has passed. Our two lands always knew harmony, until greed and selfishness took hold of two hearts.*
>
> *One heart belonged to an elven king. He started out as a wise and caring leader. People looked to him to fix their problems. His rule began with compassion, but all too soon, his darker side took hold.*

The other heart was of a human queen, who was always corrupt. She lusted after beautiful things to help hide her blackened soul.

In public, they both appeared kind and gracious, but when no others were looking, the evils of their heart took over.

On the island of our two nations, in a sacred place, was a large stone. The stone held great worth to the greedy, but some believed its magical powers were more precious than any treasure. Legend said the stone was created when humans and elves made a pact to always love and respect one another. Its magic powers were to grow strong with the growth of love between the two peoples.

Many would come to visit the stone's resting place, to get a glimpse of what helped strengthen the two nations. Very few saw it for its monetary value in the beginning, but as time passed, more and more saw it thus.

Until two people plotted to steal it for their own selfish causes.

As the weather turned cold and day gave its place to night, visitors left the sacred place. Only two guards stood watch, a human and an elf, and those were for show, for despite the greed in people, nobody believed someone would ever try to take the glittering stone.

By four cold-blooded hands, the two guards fell, and both attackers stopped to look at each other. The wicked king laughed, and the queen whose heart lusted for gold smiled. They did not plan this together, but fate intervened on their behalf.

Two greedy hands reached for the stone at the same time, each trying to grab the stone before the other. In their haste to steal it, they knocked the stone off it's base. The stone slowly slipped to the ground, as if many hands tried to catch it. But none could. The sacred stone landed on hard marble with a sickening crash.

The greedy nobles saw with great delight that the stone had split evenly in two. They looked at each other and came to a silent agreement. Each grabbed the half closest to them and ran off before another soul should know they were there.

Soon it was discovered that the guards were murdered and the sacred stone was missing. Small bickerings started between the two nations, quickly escalating to large fights. The precious stone was never heard of again. Most forgot about the love the magic stone had supposedly helped create.

Now we are looking to war. Hearts everywhere are heavy. It is told by a wise man that this war shall be one of many. After many years and long wars, the two nations will despise one another but will learn to tolerate each other again.

Our two people that were once one broke apart and change came upon them. Magic diminished in one people and then slowly in the other. They lost that which was more dear than magic —the knowledge of them being one. Humans and Elves grew to think themselves separate, when they are in fact no more different than a blue-eyed person is from a green-eyed one.

But hope shall come. An elven princess with a pure heart will shun selfish desires for the good of her people and will wed a human prince whose heart is full of care and love.

Their love and mercy shall spread throughout the land. Hearts shall begin to mend. The two halves of the sacred stone shall be found. These two people shall have the power to reunite the two halves, restoring loving magic to the land.

This is the only hope I have left for my people, for now their hearts are hardened to see wise ways.

It's a lot to take in. I'm not sure where to start. One thing I do know is I'm grateful we took the time to find this. But it's not all as easy as finding the third scroll.

"Can you believe we were once one people?" Robert says. "That our two races aren't so different after all?"

"Try convincing the elves and humans of that," Andries says. "I've been working among both of them most of my life, and I doubt they'll ever accept such a thing."

"But they're making progress," I say. Humans and elves, the same race, at least at one time. "Just the fact that humans and elves are working here together is progress."

"We do need to do what we can to bring them together," Robert says.

"Another question—how are we ever going to find a rock that was broken and stolen thousands of years ago?" I ask.

"I don't know that we can. Not without some type of clue, like we had for the scrolls."

"But we have to. We can't let our people stay torn apart because we can't find a stupid rock."

"We'll figure something out," Robert says, rubbing my back.

But for all we know, the rock is gone forever, and our people will never truly get along, though we now know they should be one.

Chapter
TWENTY-NINE

AFTER THE REVELATION and new challenge of the scroll, I don't have much of an appetite. Still, we sit down to eat a meal together. Robert's at my side, Jocleyn on my other side, as well as both human and elf workers. It would be nicer if it wasn't with a group of other people, but I suppose that's what after the wedding is for. Bringing our people together. Well, sometimes. We'll always be royalty and will always have people want to spend time with us.

Not that I mind spending time with the people, but for once, I'd like some alone time with my betrothed. Some day soon we'll have more alone time.

We'll be staying at both of our castles, traveling around until a new castle can be built. Though maybe we should just rule from this one. Humans and elves are working to build it together after all. Why not make it our castle? It's something to think about anyway.

"What do you think about having a once a-week meal with some of the people after we're married?" I ask Robert.

"I think that sounds like a wonderful plan. I bet the people would really enjoy that."

"And it'd be a great way for us to get to know them better."

It'd also be a great way for those who want to take your life to get in the palace," Stewart says.

"Oh, I'm sure you can find those people and sort them out."

"It's not always that easy." His sigh says a lot.

Robert coughs. And then coughs again and again.

"Are you all right?" I ask.

For a moment he says nothing, and then he gives a fourth cough and starts pulling at the neck of his shirt while shaking his head.

"Robert." I jump up. "Are you choking?"

He shakes his head, face going pale. His breathing grows rapid. I check his pulse to find it going fast. He points at his food and coughs, but he shook his head about choking.

A worse thought enters my mind. "I think he's been poisoned." I look at his food and turn back to him. "Someone has to save him."

Jocelyn hurries to her feet and rushes out the room, presumably to get help.

An elf from clear across the room jumps up and runs toward us. "What happened?"

"I think he ate something poisoned." Tears are fighting to come to my eyes, but now's not the time to lose control. I have to stay levelheaded for this. "What do we do?"

"I'm a healer," the elf says. "Stand back."

He helps Robert to the floor and lays him on his side. By this time, Robert's eyes are fluttering, and his hands are fisting up.

"Try to keep calm," the elf says to him.

Robert continues to sputter. My heart yanks me to the ground beside them. "What can I do to help?"

"Are you healthy?"

"Yes."

"Then give me your hand."

I put my hand in his while he touches Robert on the shoulder. Not a second later, I feel the pull on my own magic. My health. He's using my health, and from moving around, I can tell he's using some of his own to heal Robert. Are we too late?

I search for all my health, every part of me that's whole and good, and I shove it to where I'm holding hands with the healer, helping make the process go faster.

Robert coughs, and then stops breathing.

"No." I put my free hand on his cheek. My vision blurs with tears. "Don't you dare leave me."

The elf jerks my health in one quick blow. I chase my magic after it, wanting both to help and to know what he's doing. I accompany him straight through to his hand, to Robert's shoulder, and to Robert's heart. There's a quick flash of magic, and Robert's heart starts beating again.

I want to sigh with relief, but there's still the poison to deal with. I can feel it in there, damaging his body. No matter how many times this elf can restart his heart, it will do no good if there's the poison in him.

But then the healer's magic is off in every direction. I follow what I can, though I'm not fast enough to follow it all.

It's spreading throughout Robert's body, attacking the poison, overloading it with good health. It's not enough, though; I feel the poison slowly killing Robert. I want to cry out. Instead, I work on helping the healer as best I can. It's not enough, though.

"I need another healthy person willing to help," the elf calls out. "Quick."

To my surprise, a human steps forward. A man. "I'll help."

"Touch my shoulder."

The man puts a hand on the elf's shoulder and the elf starts pulling on his health as well. With the three of us combined, there's a sense of maybe making it. Soon, another elf joins us and puts a hand on the healer's back. A human woman does the same. Then there's a crowd around us, as many people as possible connecting with the healer. Jocelyn brings in an elf. They both take a look at the situation and grab on to the crowd around us.

Tears roll down my cheeks as the healer uses the health of all those touching him to heal Robert. To chase away every last speck of poison.

And then it's gone.

Robert's going to be all right, and it's because of both elves and humans.

Chapter
THIRTY
◟

"HOW DID THIS HAPPEN?" I ask. "I thought with Captain Smythe in prison the attempts on your life would stop."

"It appears I still have enemies." Robert looks pale as he lies down on the sofa in one of the sitting rooms.

How can we fight an enemy we don't know? "Thank goodness for the elf that saved your life. Without him…"

"I'm fine, though it was a frightening attempt."

"Too close for my comfort, in the very least." I take his hand into mine. "Much too close. We'll have to give that elf some type of honor."

"He can be my best man."

I smile and rest my head against his shoulder. "Promise me you'll be careful. With someone out for you, I'm extra worried."

"I'll be as safe as I can while still living my life," I say. "The renovations are almost complete." That's one thing to look forward to—our wedding day is almost here.

"Maybe that's why they took another chance at trying to kill me."

"I'm afraid it's not going to be over when we get married," I say.

"We've dealt with it in the past. We'll have to deal with it in the future."

"I think we should get you a personal taster."

He groans. "I don't want someone else's life on the line just because I might be poisoned."

"But they're trained for it. They can detect it better than a regular person can, and they know how to deal with it when it happens. I think it would be for the best."

He sighs. "You're right. I just hate having to go through all this."

I give his hand a squeeze. "I know. But we can't have the future king of Bardus and Omanska taking such risks."

"You're right," he says. "It's hard putting another's life ahead of my own by having a taster."

"We'll be extra cautious." With a taster in place, I hope there'll be no more problems.

"Who do you think is still after me and possibly you?"

"I don't know." Thoughts of the past year race through my mind. "You know, the strange thing is there haven't been attempts on my life. Well, there was that one guy who attacked me in the castle, but he came in through a room filled with guards and sword fighters. He didn't have a chance at making it. Everyone else has tried to kidnap me or threaten me against marrying a human. Even when fighting, they seemed cautious around me. They might try to injure me but not take my life. It's only you and Abner that were at any real risk."

"Do you think the arrow that hit Abner was meant for him? That was clearly an attack on your life."

"I don't know."

"You do know. You think whoever is trying to kill me is an elf, don't you?"

I sigh. "I don't want to think one of my own people could do it, but I'm afraid it is one of them. I don't understand why."

"Maybe we never will."

I hope no attempt actually takes his life. The more they increase in frequency, though, the more likely one of them is to succeed, and a life without Robert would be no life at all.

WE SEARCH LIKE MAD for the poisoner. Stewart leads a group searching through the entire castle and island. Robert is resting with several guards at his side. Stewart insists that I stay close to him while he searches. The good thing is that it means I'll be able to know everything that's going on.

Teams of three are sent to search together. Jocelyn and Emeline go together, which surprises me. They take a guard with them, just in case someone is lurking out there. I just didn't expect Jocelyn to forgive Emeline, but I suppose if I can, she can too.

Stewart, another guard, and I are searching through a guest room.

"What are we looking for?" I ask Stewart.

"Anything that could be poison or links a person with trying to hurt Robert." His voice is stern, though I know it's not directed at me. Sometime when all this had been happening, Stewart had grown to care for Robert too, like a father.

As I search in a drawer of papers, looking them over to make certain they don't contain anything incriminatory, I ask, "Why do you think someone would want to hurt Robert?"

"There's lots of reasons. Unless we find the person who poisoned him, we may never know."

That spurs my search on harder. I don't want to be left not knowing why. "These papers are all innocuous." I want to slam them back in the drawer, but these are someone's personal papers, so instead, I make a neat pile out of them. "Has anyone not agreed to have their room and belongings searched?"

"Everyone agreed. Which means it's unlikely that we're going to find anything in the castle, but we have to look anyway."

I move to the bed, where I look under the pillows. "Do you think they'll find anything outside of the castle?"

"It's hard to say."

After a thorough search of the bed turns up nothing, I don't know where else to look. We've scoured this room through and through. While we've been working, teams have come in reporting to Stewart that they haven't been able to find anything either.

Jocelyn, Emeline, and their guard enter the room.

"Were you able to find anything?" I ask.

Jocelyn shakes her head. "I wish we had, but we turned up nothing. I'm so sorry, Arabella."

"You searched. That's what matters." But really, I'm disappointed. How are we ever going to find an almost murderer if he didn't leave any clues behind?

"I have a thought," Emeline says.

"What's that?" Stewart asks.

"Maybe we should question everyone. See what we can find out that way."

"It's a good idea," he says. "Let's get started on it."

I help gather everyone together. There's some grumbling, but not much of it when I explain it's because of my safety and Robert's. That seems to calm them down. Stewart interviews them one-by-one. It takes hours to get through everyone, and what's worse, there seems to be no sign of success.

When Jocelyn and I are left out standing alone with a guard, I say, "I can't believe this isn't working."

"I thought it would too. Someone should know something."

"The fact that they don't makes me feel like we're in more danger than I first thought."

She frowns. "Do you really think it's that bad?"

"I do. I hope we don't have to cancel the wedding because of it."

"Don't you dare cancel," she says, passion in her voice. "That's what this person, whoever they are, wants. You can't give into them now."

"You're right." I sigh. "It's hard with Robert being so sick."

"I know, but everything's going to turn out fine. You'll see."

The door to the room Stewart is using to interrogate people opens, and an elf steps out, hurrying away.

"Jocelyn," Stewart calls.

"You don't need to talk to her," I say. "I'm certain she had nothing to do with it."

"I believe you," he says. "But we need to try everything, and so far I haven't gotten any information. She's the last one left."

Jocelyn steps forward. "I'm happy to talk to Stewart. Anything I can do to help Robert."

She goes in the room, and the door closes. I wait in front of it, drumming my fingers on my leg. I can't handle the waiting. I know Jocelyn didn't do anything, but what if Stewart thinks she did? What if he thinks she's behind it?

My nerves are frayed. This has all been too much.

It's only a little while later that the door opens and Jocelyn comes out, Stewart at her side.

"Arabella, I'd like to talk to you," he says.

Jocelyn gives me a quick hug, and I enter the room with Stewart. He closes the door, and I take a seat. I feel bad for everyone that has been in this seat before me. Except for the poisoner. I don't feel bad for him at all.

"Did you find any news?"

Stewart sits across from me. "Nothing. It's like the culprit just disappeared."

"Is anyone missing?"

"Not as far as I can tell."

I slouch back in my chair. "What about his food? Did anyone have any contact with it?"

"Just the kitchen staff, but they did admit to leaving it unattended."

"You don't think one of them did it, do you?"

He shakes his head. "Not as far as I can tell. They all seem innocent."

"That's the problem. Everyone does," I say.

"Until we figure out who's behind this, I want you both guarded at all times."

I nod. I have no problem with the request. "What about our food?"

"I'll have a two guards over it at all times too. We'll make sure no one can tamper with it again."

I think this over and decide it's well thought out. With two guards over it, they'd both have to be against us to do something bad. "Thanks for all your hard work, Stewart."

"It's what I'm here for."

That and more. Thank goodness for Stewart.

Chapter
THIRTY-ONE
∿

THE MORNING IS GOING WELL. The renovations are almost done, notes are being sent out to invite people to the wedding, and there's been nothing but peace since Robert was last attacked.

His attack. That's the last thing I want to think about. The only good thing that came of it was humans and elves coming together, to heal him. Since I've known him, there have been too many close calls, especially recently.

Is this really going to be how things are done the rest of our lives? I sure hope not.

"What are you thinking about?" Stewart asks.

I sigh, looking around the room I'm to approve of this morning. I was so lost in thought I almost forgot what I was supposed to be doing. It looks good. The wooden floors are gleaming, the fireplace is in good repair, the bedclothes are freshly laundered, and the window has been fixed. It's all good to go, but not what I was thinking about. "Just all the times someone had tried to kill Robert since I've known him."

"It's been scary for you, hasn't it?"

Scary is an understatement. "It has. I don't know how much more of this I can handle."

"You can do this, Arabella. You can take whatever anyone throws at you."

"Do you really think so?"

"I know so. You're stronger than you believe."

Which brings me to another thought. "And what about my looks? Do you think it matters that I look different? That I'm stuck somewhere between an elf and a human?"

"You are better off than you know. It's the perfect place to put yourself in to unite two races."

I slouch. "But I don't feel very beautiful."

"Beauty is what you wish to see."

"I don't know what I wish to see. I only know how others react toward me." Especially my own mother. No matter how much time passes, she doesn't seem to be able to come to terms with how I look now.

I change topics to get my mind off of it. "Do you have any family?"

He gives me a smile. "Just you."

"I'm truly grateful you're here. You've helped me through so much."

"It's been my pleasure. When I started out serving your family as a boy, I didn't think that I would wind up finding such a wonderful young woman to serve."

"You're too kind. Besides, I remember being a kid. I wasn't always the easiest to watch over."

He chuckles. "I remember when Constance couldn't find you. Turned out you were playing hide and seek and you chose to hide under the king's throne."

"You're just lucky I stayed in the castle." Thoughts of Constance still hurt, but not as much as they did at first. "I miss her."

"I miss her too. She was a good woman."

"Fire," someone yells. "Fire!"

I head toward the commotion.

"Wrong way, Arabella," Stewart says, gently clasping my arm.

I hesitate. "We have to go help."

"The best way you can help is by getting out of danger."

He's right. Unfortunately. I follow him outside. Once we are some distance from the building, I turn to look. Flames are shooting out one room of the castle.

"Do you know whose room that is?"

Stewart is silent.

"You know and you're not telling me. Please say it's not Robert's."

"It's not Robert's."

I give a sigh of relief. That's one piece of good news. But by the way Stewart is standing, body tense and hand on his sword, I know something is wrong. "Whose room is it?"

"It's Andries."

The flames take on new meaning. I stare at them, horrified. "You don't think he's still in there, do you?"

"I don't know."

"We have to help."

"You can't go in there," Stewart says. "The last thing we need is for you to put yourself in danger. Laws forbid something actually happen to you."

I want to stomp my foot on the ground. Instead, I settle for twisting my hand in my dress. "I know, all right? I know. But I can't stand by when one of my friends is in danger like this. There has to be something I can do."

He shakes his head.

"I know. What if I made it rain?"

"Do it."

I waste no time in pulling my magic together and sending it shooting at the clouds. It's difficult, but I minimize it to around the castle, so there will be fewer consequences for the spell. Much needed water pours down.

They are fighting it from the inside too, I hope. I let it pour as long as it needs to, directing it through the window.

"Aren't you getting tired yet?" Stewart asks. "I think the flames have died down."

"I'm fine. I can keep it up longer." In truth, I feel as if I could keep it up indefinitely, should I want to. Who knows what type of consequence that would create, though?

Sometime later, after we can no longer see flames, a servant runs out to me. "The fire has been stopped," she says.

I pull my magic back and stop the torrent of rain. "Is everyone safe? How's Andries? My mother? Robert?" There are more people I want to ask after, but she looks pale, making me afraid of what the answer might be.

"They're all safe, no one was hurt, but I was told to send for you as quickly as possible."

A huge release of tension flows from me. Whatever the problem is, it can't be as bad someone being hurt or dying because of this fire.

With that thought of relief, I follow the servant girl to the castle and to a small room, Stewart at my side. People are huddled around the door. Many I recognize from their help around the castle. How much longer is this going to make our wedding take? It better not delay us by too much. I'm past ready to marry Robert.

Thinking of him seems to bring him to me. He pulls me into a hug. "I was worried about you."

"And I was worried about you," I say, wrapping my arms around him. We have an audience, but I don't really care. He is about to be my husband.

He pulls away but doesn't let go of my hand. "You're not going to like what's in there." He motions to the closed door I know leads to a small room. Two guards are among the people gathered around it.

"What is in there?" I ask.

"The person that started the fire."

I don't wait for more. I turn, march straight for the door, and open it up.

In the middle of the room, looking as angry as I've ever seen her, is Emeline.

Chapter
THIRTY-TWO

❦

"**W**HAT HAVE YOU DONE?**"** I demand of Emeline.

"You didn't really buy all that garbage I told you, did you? I mean—come on—who cares if they're friends with the high and mighty Princess Arabella?"

Her words stab at me, making me wish we'd never had that conversation back at the Pomum Heart library. I should have known better than to forgive her, but I thought she changed. Hoped she did. "I don't care if you want to be my friend," I say. "I do care that you're making bad decisions. You know nothing can make your sentence lighter this time, right?"

"After what Octavian went through, this is the least you deserve."

"Octavian brought on his own punishment. And what do you think I deserve?"

"To have the scrolls you cared about so dearly destroyed. You cared more about them than you did about Octavian. I made sure there's nothing more you can do with them."

I shrug. She must not have known they were just copies. "I only wanted to learn about our people. It had nothing to do with Octavian. He set his own trap with his actions, and now you've set yours. One thing I have to know. Did you poison Robert?"

She laughs, a maniacal one that has me cringing.

"I'll take that as a yes," I say. "Are you working with anyone else?"

"I don't need to," she says. "Humans and elves fight enough among themselves without me attaching myself to anyone. The one I want is gone."

Tears leak from her eyes, but I have no sympathy toward her. At least not for the situation she's put herself in. I do feel sorry that she's chosen such a bad path to go down.

"Guards?" I call out.

The two guards pop their head in the door. One of them says, "Yes, my lady?"

"Please take her to the dungeon. We'll have my father deal with her once he arrives." Mother will probably help, but my father tends to deal with punishments more than her. I look straight at Emeline. "I assure you he won't be lenient. He was once. You don't get a second chance. Not with your actions and attitude."

Her nostrils flare, but she doesn't say another word as the guards lead her out of the room.

"You handled that well," Robert says.

"Yes," my mother says, coming in from the hall, not making eye contact with me. "She did."

"Thank you for you kind words. Both of you." The spectators are still there, so I close the door. After my talk with Stewart, I can't wait longer to speak to her about this. "Mother, I have to ask you something."

"Go on."

My hands shake, but I know better than to clench them together or twist them in my dress in front of her. Especially when I'm trying to make a good impression. When I have to say something I wish I didn't need to. "Mother, why won't you look at me?"

Robert moves to my side and puts his hand on the small of my back.

"I don't know what you're talking about." But she still won't make eye contact with me.

"Ever since I disguised myself like a human and became more humanlike, you won't give me the smallest of glances." She also called me *hideous*, but that's not something I want to bring up.

She holds her head higher. "I know it's not the best way to handle things, but you have to understand how difficult it is for me to look at you, when you're so… different."

"Different, yes, but I'm not less of a person. I don't even think I'm ugly." Not any longer. "I'm an elf with more humanlike features. I realized my kids will be the same, with me marrying a human prince." The thought of having children with Robert makes me blush, but I press forward. "They're going to need their grandmother to look at them. I hope you can overcome my looks to make that happen."

She doesn't look at me. "I promise you I will look at my grandchildren."

The passion with which she speaks makes me believe her. Why then, will she still not look at me?

Chapter
THIRTY-THREE

I'M WORKING ON THE GARDEN with Robert at my side when a woman calls his name.

He gets on his feet and rushes toward the woman, whom I recognize as his mother, Teresa. She's surrounded by an entourage of guards and servants. She looks like quite the statement, having even more guards than I do.

I was wondering when she'd make it here. I was beginning to worry something happened to her ship, but in reality, she was probably working. As important as this wedding is, I'm sure her work is just as important.

As they hug, I stand and brush the dirt off my hands. My knees want to shake with this new development. I met her before, but now it's as her future daughter-in-law. Of course, I have to be covered in dirt at this moment. It's a good thing Mother isn't here to witness it.

She turns to me. "And here we are again. I didn't realize when last we met that I was talking to my future daughter-in-law."

I almost gasp aloud when she gathers me into her arms as she did Robert a moment ago. Despite the surprise, it feels safe enough. My future mother-in-law, a merchant. I wouldn't have it any other way, but I wonder if my mother knows. Father shouldn't care, as long as Robert is a prince.

When Teresa pulls back, she discreetly wipes off the dirt she gained from hugging me. It's not easy working in a garden and staying princess-like.

A man with green eyes steps forward but otherwise looks like an older version of Robert.

"This is my father, Dale," Robert says.

I give him a crusty hand. "It's a pleasure to meet you, sir."

"No need to be so formal," he says. "We're going to be family soon."

"I'm so glad to be here with you both," Teresa says. "How can I help the wedding plans go smoothly for you?"

Though she's asking with what sounds like sincere intent, she's looking at my garden like she hopes she doesn't have to work in it.

"Nothing, really. Preparations are about complete," I say. "We're waiting for some more guests. The best thing you can do is get settled. We would love it if you'd both join us for dinner."

"That I can happily manage." By the smile on her lips, I'm certain that's the case. This evening is sure to be an entertaining one.

"Let me show you to your room," I say.

She glances at my feet and then Robert's. They're covered in dirt. "I can show myself in. One of the servants will take us to my room."

"If you're certain?" Robert asks.

"Of course. I wanted to have a look at the renovations they've made to this castle, anyway. I'm in the market for something like this."

"We have been for a while now," Dale says.

"Well, it's time to get serious," she replies.

After a quick hug to Robert, they hurry away. Too bad Sulamay Island isn't for sale, and it won't be as long as I have a say in its future.

Robert moves to my side. "She means well."

"She's fine. How come your mother isn't next in line for the throne?"

"Because the lineage is through my father's side and he abdicated his title long ago when he married my mother."

"Do you think she wishes it was otherwise?"

He runs a hand across his jaw. "I don't think so. She always wants more stuff, it seems, but I think that's only for things. I don't think she'd want to be ruling over people."

"And do you?"

"I don't want to lord over them. Instead, I'd like to help them, like we've talked about."

I wrap my hand in his, intertwining our fingers. We belong together, and together we shall be.

Chapter

THIRTY-FOUR

༄

T HE WEDDING IS TOMORROW. I've never been
so excited for something in all my life. It's almost
here, and nothing is going to stop it from happening. Absolutely nothing.

Octavian is dead. Captain Smythe is in prison, surrounded
by a dozen of our men, sentenced to death. Emeline has been
captured. The only skirmishes left are minor and don't have
to do with my wedding.

I find Robert in a sitting room, staring out the window at
the ocean. Stewart leaves us for once, letting us spend some
time together before we wed. "Fancy seeing you here," I tell
Robert.

He takes my hand. "Everything is ready. And think of all
the people who've come."

"I can't believe how many humans and elves have shown
up. It's more than I would have guessed."

"I know. As long as no fights break out, we'll have the perfect wedding."

"Don't jinx us now."

He wraps me into a hug. "Nothing is going to stand in our way tomorrow."

"That's exactly what I was thinking."

He pulls away. "I need to head out."

"Where are you going?"

"Your mother asked to meet me."

"What about?" I ask.

"Wedding stuff, I'm sure."

"I wonder what she's going to tell you. Can I come?"

"You are probably not supposed to." He smiles at me. "But I can't resist you. Why don't you come along, and then you can leave before she tells me what she needs to."

"Sounds good."

We walk outside, toward the island's small lake. It's a beautiful day. Maybe after we're done speaking to Mother, I'll go for a swim. If she allows it, which she may if there's no one else around.

Holding hands with my beloved is nice. The trees are heavy with green leaves, flowers bloom, and birds twitter about. If tomorrow is anything like this, it will be the perfect wedding day.

We find Mother standing next to some trees near the lake. Her face is as serene as the water is still.

Robert greets her.

"Mother, I'm so happy to see you," I say.

"And I you, though I admit, I am somewhat surprised."

"I know I'm not supposed to be here while you talk with Robert. I thought I'd walk him over."

"Without a chaperone?"

I feel chagrined. "I should have grabbed Jocelyn. I'm sorry. But all of that will be over tomorrow. Here, I'll go and leave you to talk."

"No, no. You might as well stay and hear what I have to say to Robert."

"Are you certain?"

"Positive. This is something you need to hear as well. I was planning on speaking with you separately, but now will do just as well. Come stand by me, please."

"Of course." I give Robert's hand a squeeze and then leave his side to stand by my mother. She's so graceful and elegant, even out here in the woods. She's definitely fitting the part of a queen.

"Robert," she says, "come closer."

He steps forward until he's only a couple of paces away. I watch her, anxious to hear what she has to say. Hopefully she hasn't constructed some surprise wedding dress for me like what I had when I almost married before. That seems like so long ago now. And I like the dress I designed myself. I'd hate to have to give it up.

"It's time I tell you something," she says.

There's a snap from the left of us. I whip my gaze toward the sound, and Aiden shows up through the thicket of trees.

I draw my sword. "What are you doing here? You're supposed to be in prison."

Robert pulls out his sword as well. We both face Aiden, trying to protect my mother from him. He holds up his hands, palm forward, like he doesn't mean us harm, but I don't trust him. Not for a moment.

"I was let out," he says.

"Let out?" Robert asks. "By whom? Your sentence was for years."

"It doesn't matter. I escaped. But I wanted to get to you and say I'm sorry. I'm on your side."

"What do you think you are doing, Aiden?" Mother sounds more authoritative than either Robert or me.

"I had to come. I had to tell Arabella—"

"That's Princess Arabella to you," Mother demands.

"I had to tell the Princess that I'm on her side."

"Clearly," I say.

"No. I mean it. I'm on your side."

"If you're on my side, I want you to come over here and let me hold this sword to you."

He eyes my blade. "That sounds more like a threat than a way to make you believe me."

"If you won't go to her," Robert says, "then I'll hold a sword to you, and I won't be nearly as nice as she is."

"I don't believe that for a minute. Neither of you would hurt someone if you could help it," Aiden says. He seems to consider for a moment, then adds, "Fine, then. I'll prove myself to you."

He slowly walks over, hands held in the air, until he reaches me. When he stops at the level of my sword, I breathe a sigh of relief. Only… "If you knew I was going to send you back to prison, why did you come all the way over here? Why not go for freedom somewhere else?" I ask.

"As I told you, I'm on your side."

"On my side, how?"

"We should get him back to the guards before we do any sort of questioning," Mother says. "What if he tries to escape?"

"But he came here willingly." Something doesn't add up. My arm begins to shake. I lower my sword, but I'm ready to pounce it back up at the slightest movement.

"Robert, check him for weapons, though we all know his greatest weapon is the power to nullify magic."

Robert quickly checks him over. "No weapons."

"See? I'm harmless. Now if I could—"

"You're anything but harmless," Mother says. "We all know how you treated Arabella in Bardus."

"Yes, but—"

"There are no buts."

"Fine. Why don't you tell them, Your Majesty?"

I turn to my mother. "What's he talking about?"

When she says nothing, Aiden adds, "Yes. What exactly am I talking about?"

Suddenly, she whisks the sword from Robert's hand and holds it to Robert's throat. "You can't marry him."

"Mother?" My stomach drops.

"I'm sorry, Arabella. I know you've fallen in love with him, but he couldn't make you happy. It's not possible. A human and an elf were never meant to be together."

"Yes, we are. Those scrolls—"

"Scrolls." She harrumphs. "What do they know? They're ancient history. They know nothing. We should be wiping out the human race, not trying to unite with them."

Fear quickens my heartbeat. Wipe out the human race? What is she talking about? "Mother, please drop the sword."

Instead, she tries to press it farther into Robert. I parry her attack and jump in front of him, leaving Aiden to the side. Who cares if he gets away? "No one can hurt the man I love," I say. "Not even you, Mother."

"Haven't you been listening?" She drops her usual poise as she advances on me, sword in hand. "You can't marry him."

"But you arranged our betrothal."

"No, that was your father. When you were a little child, your father was so set on it. Nothing I could say would persuade him to change his mind. He had to unite our two races. He couldn't see those humans for what they really are."

"Mother, you're scaring me."

"Good. You should be scared. Nothing else fazed you. Not death threats. Oh, no—keep to the wedding. Not sending pirates after you and killing your guard. Not having Captain Smythe kidnap you from your own wedding. Not having Aiden attack you. Not even that human who tried to shoot you. He was going to miss, of course, but when Prince Phillip jumped in front of the arrow, I thought it was perfect. No more wedding.

"But you came home full of ideas on how everything was going to be. How you would marry the new prince and make my nightmares a reality. So I sent pirates after him again and again, to kill him." She advances on me. "Every time, you had to stand in the way. And then you captured my best weapon. Captain Smythe."

"Captain Smythe was working for you?" My heart feels as if it's breaking in a million pieces.

"Of course. You didn't think he cared about politics without being paid in some way."

"I can't believe you did that. How could you?" This can't be happening. I knew Mother wasn't perfect, but this? It can't possibly be, except it's coming from her lips.

"It was easier than you believe," she says. "Now step aside, so I can finish him off myself."

"Like either of us will let you," I say. "Even being the queen won't save you from the crimes you've committed."

I back against Robert, letting him support me. It's the strength I need to fight an enemy I didn't know I had.

My own mother.

Chapter
THIRTY-FIVE

"COME ON, ARABELLA," Mother says. "Let me through."

I swallow past the thickening in my throat. "I can't let you. You know I can't."

I keep Aiden in my peripheral vision as she takes a step forward. I hold up my sword toward her, though shakily. For the first time since my features changed, she looks at me straight in the eye. "You will let me past, right this instant."

"I can't do that."

She steps forward again, and my sword wavers. It's not that I want her to get to Robert; it's that she's still my mother. I can't imagine taking the blade to her.

She lifts her sword, reaching past me with the blade. I feel Robert back away. Aiden doesn't move. Is he going to help or hinder?

I point my sword back at her. "Leave him alone."

"As long as he's going to marry you, I can't do that."

"He's the man I love. Why can't you let us be?"

She takes another step forward. I take two steps back and try to knock the sword from her hand. She has a better hold on it than I expected.

The surprise must show on my face because she says, "You weren't the only one who practiced sword fighting when you were younger."

Fear grips my chest. If she's willing to fight me, I don't know if I can stop her. That she's my mother would make this the fiercest fight I've ever been in. Captain Smythe has nothing on her.

She thrusts her sword toward my shoulder, but I block it.

"Get out of my way," she says. "I don't want to hurt you, but I will if that's what it takes to get to him."

"This is insane. You can't attack me."

She thrusts toward me again.

"Mother, stop."

Her full dress doesn't even slow her down. If only I'd brought Jocelyn and Stewart with me. I'd send her for help while he guarded me and Robert.

What would Stewart be doing now? I know. He would pretend this was any other fight. He wouldn't let who she is stop him.

Aiden rushes forward.

I don't even think. I just send an electric spark through me. He falls to the ground, and behind me there's a crash. Robert was too close to me. I knocked him out as well. I curse myself, but there's not time to think on it. Mother is heading toward Robert's prone form. I skate around Aiden and focus on just her.

I feel the ground beneath my feet, strong and firm, and let my legs become an extension of it. I take that strength and move it all the way through me until my sword is steady. It doesn't make a difference that my opponent is skilled; she hasn't fought as recently as I have. I can best her, and I can do it without seriously injuring her.

I jab my sword forward, and she jumps back. We go back and forth, fighting, our swords clanging and skirts swishing. Everything else becomes a blur around me as I focus on her. Numerous times, her blade comes close to me, but I manage to block it.

No matter how many times I try to strike her, I can't bring myself to do it. It doesn't matter what I try to tell myself; she's still my mother.

The swords continue to fly through the air. No matter which way I go, Mother continues to attack me. She fights harder, and I'm losing ground. I don't have the heart to battle her—it's not in me. But neither will I let her harm Robert.

Out of nowhere, Aiden rushes forward, reaches out, and touches Mother. The world stills.

Mother's beautiful face, the one I'm used to seeing my entire life, melts away into a hideous, scary thing. Something that's not even an elf. Sunken eyes, a nose that's barely there, skin wrinkled beyond anything I've ever seen before, and a jagged snarl.

Mother screeches and swats at Aiden's arm. I put my sword to her throat, stopping her frantic thrashings.

"Mother?" I ask. "Is that you?"

"Yes." Her voice is as graceful as ever, at odds with the ghastly thing it's coming out of. "Why couldn't you just let things be? Why did you have to go and ruin everything?"

Robert stands, coming to the side of me.

"What happened to you?" I ask her.

"What happened is that I did what you should have done. I've used a spell all these years to keep my beauty. Everyone knows me for my looks, but you wouldn't listen. When you first grew ugly, I tried to tell you to keep yourself spelled all the time, to hide the repulsiveness you brought on yourself, but you wouldn't do it."

"You're making me grateful I didn't," I say, still staring at her in shock.

"You should have. Appearances are everything."

I shake my head. "In trying to gain what you wanted most, you lost it."

"No. As soon as Aiden lets me go, I'll have it back."

I eye Aiden, wondering what his game is. Whose side he's really on.

"It's not real. None of it," I tell her. I focus in on Aiden. "Whose side are you on?"

"I'm on your side."

I want to believe him, want to think that he's telling the truth, but I have no reason to trust him other than him coming to tell me about Mother. Even that, I'm not sure of. How can I trust anyone? After I let myself trust Emeline, that went bad. I don't want that happening again.

"Why did you listen to the queen at first?" I ask him.

His features scrunch with regret. "I thought she was right. I thought that humans and elves should never be together.

I was willing to sacrifice so much for it, even help Captain Smythe because she asked me to. I tried to stop your marriage at every turn, but you persisted on. That persistence and the way you and Robert were together made me think things differently once I had time to think about it."

"It's hard to trust that's true after everything you've done."

"I know, but I promise I'll try."

It's probably the best answer I'm going to get out of him now. And Mother. What to do about her? I'm not sure so I turn to Robert.

"What do we do about this?"

"I don't know. I've never dealt with anything like this before."

"And she's not your mother."

He puts a hand on my shoulder, comforting me.

"Get your hand off her," the woman I once considered my mother screams.

"No. He can touch me whenever he likes. And we're getting married tomorrow. No matter how you try to stop us, we will be together. We will unite our races."

She does something then that I've never seen her do before. She breaks down and cries.

THIRTY-SIX

I T TAKES US a while to get back to the castle. At first, she fights us every step of the way. When I tell Aiden to let go of her, her beauty comes back. Fake though it is, this seems to calm her enough to keep going, though Aiden stays close in case we need him. Not that I trust him, but I can deal with that later.

When we reach the castle, I send the first person I see for my father, saying he's to meet us in a private room.

I try to be discreet with my sword, forcing the queen there. I can't chance her getting away at this point—she's caused too much damage to be let loose—but I also don't want to cause a scene until I know what to do with her.

We only have to wait in the room a few long, agonizing minutes before Father shows up.

He opens the door, his expression one of angry confusion. "What is going on in here?" he asks.

"Please close the door behind you." I sound much calmer than I feel. He does what I ask, and I motion to a chair. "Why don't you sit down?"

"I will, after you tell me why in all that's holy you are holding a sword to your mother and letting a known felon go free. Rumors are flying all over the castle."

"I really think it would be best if you sat down. Robert, would you..." I don't have to finish my sentence. He grabs the chair and brings it over for my father to sit in. Though Father still stands, I feel better knowing it's nearby.

"I have a story to tell you, and it's not going to be easy for me to say or for you to hear."

I've only gone a line in, when my father sits down. Aiden and Robert stay close. I hurry on, and by the time I finish my story, he's pale.

"Is this true?" Father's voice is quiet, but it pierces the room as he faces my mother.

"If only you'd listened to me when you first betrothed Arabella to the human prince, we wouldn't be here," she replies.

My father shakes his head over and over. When he stops, he looks even more lost than I feel. "How could you do this? I've been working so hard. All this time, I knew you were selfish and cared only about your looks, but I didn't know you could be so cruel to your own daughter."

This stirs her to life. "Cruel? It's because I love her so much and want what's best for her. There's nothing I wish for more than to love and cherish her, but you had to keep throwing her to the humans until she loved them too."

My father puts his head in his hands. When he finally looks up, he says, "Aiden, would you be so kind as to cast your anti-magic spell on my wife?"

"Of course." Aiden gives a bow to my father and then moves to touch my mother.

She jumps up screaming, but I point my sword at her again, and she settles down enough for Aiden to touch her. She appears like something out of a nightmare. Something not at all elfish or human.

As much as I don't care what someone looks like, knowing she's done this to herself trying to be as beautiful as possible makes it all the more frightening. She is, without a doubt, the scariest thing I've ever seen. Despite everything, I still love her, even if she had misguided ideas about how to help me through life. No matter what she's done to me, I'll always love her. She's my mother. But that doesn't mean I'll ever allow let her near Robert again.

Father sighs. "So this is what it comes to. You've ruined yourself over obsessing about your looks, and you've tried to ruin not just our daughter's life, but the lives of two countries because of your stupidity."

The room grows quiet.

"Aiden, please let go of my… wife."

As soon as he does so, she changes back to the form I've always known her as—the most gorgeous elf in existence. It's hard to think. What's underneath her mask doesn't matter; what's in her heart does.

And her heart's not pretty at all.

"Robert, would you please bring in the guards? After that, I would like you all to leave. I will take care of this."

Robert opens the door and ushers several guards inside, Stewart included. Then Robert and I leave. I wonder what fate will befall Aiden, but even more, I wonder what will happen to my mother.

THIRTY-SIX

~

IT TAKES US a while to get back to the castle. At first, she fights us every step of the way. When I tell Aiden to let go of her, her beauty comes back. Fake though it is, this seems to calm her enough to keep going, though Aiden stays close in case we need him. Not that I trust him, but I can deal with that later.

When we reach the castle, I send the first person I see for my father, saying he's to meet us in a private room.

I try to be discreet with my sword, forcing the queen there. I can't chance her getting away at this point—she's caused too much damage to be let loose—but I also don't want to cause a scene until I know what to do with her.

We only have to wait in the room a few long, agonizing minutes before Father shows up.

He opens the door, his expression one of angry confusion. "What is going on in here?" he asks.

"Please close the door behind you." I sound much calmer than I feel. He does what I ask, and I motion to a chair. "Why don't you sit down?"

"I will, after you tell me why in all that's holy you are holding a sword to your mother and letting a known felon go free. Rumors are flying all over the castle."

"I really think it would be best if you sat down. Robert, would you…" I don't have to finish my sentence. He grabs the chair and brings it over for my father to sit in. Though Father still stands, I feel better knowing it's nearby.

"I have a story to tell you, and it's not going to be easy for me to say or for you to hear."

I've only gone a line in, when my father sits down. Aiden and Robert stay close. I hurry on, and by the time I finish my story, he's pale.

"Is this true?" Father's voice is quiet, but it pierces the room as he faces my mother.

"If only you'd listened to me when you first betrothed Arabella to the human prince, we wouldn't be here," she replies.

My father shakes his head over and over. When he stops, he looks even more lost than I feel. "How could you do this? I've been working so hard. All this time, I knew you were selfish and cared only about your looks, but I didn't know you could be so cruel to your own daughter."

This stirs her to life. "Cruel? It's because I love her so much and want what's best for her. There's nothing I wish for more than to love and cherish her, but you had to keep throwing her to the humans until she loved them too."

Chapter
THIRTY-SEVEN
❧

IT'S A SAD REST of the day. I can't even hope that Father will still let me marry Robert tomorrow. Which feels selfish to think about, but I know how desperately our two nations need this. Plus, I want it. Mother worked so hard to stop it and started so many rumors that hurt so many people. We have to show them we can become one in peace and harmony.

But maybe it was never meant to happen. We'll never find the crystal after all—the one spoken of by the scroll. If there's no way to bring our nations together now, there may never be a way to do so. I voice all these concerns to Robert while he holds me.

The very act soothes me. I calm down enough to stay by his side. I try not to think of what must be happening behind those closed doors. What steps Father is taking to deal with someone he thought was a criminal and another person he knew as his wife.

"We need to find out how many elves were working for my mother," I tell Robert. "It seems she has a lot of people under her control."

"We will. It'll take time, but we'll find everyone."

Hours later, Father requests our presence. We meet him in a different room than before, though still a private one. It was meant to be Father and Mother's sitting room for their stay here, but it's no longer that. It's become a room of condemnation.

"Your mother has been sent to prison," he says without preamble. "She's already on a boat there. I would have given her a trial, but considering everything, I think it's best if she just goes."

"And Aiden?" I ask, trying hard not to think about what it will be like for my mother in prison. She brought this on herself; she needs to pay the consequences.

"He is going back to prison as well. Turns out he convinced one of the guards to help him escape after telling him his story. That guard will be dealt with, but not too harshly, considering the circumstances. Aiden himself will have a shortened prison sentence. While I don't believe in acting for money, he did the right thing coming forward with the truth."

"Why didn't he say something sooner?" I ask.

"Because the queen had him convinced for a while that she was right not to trust humans, but seeing you and Robert and others made him reconsider. Talking to the guard and other inmates in the jail was the final thing that did it to him."

"Too bad he couldn't have decided that a lot sooner." Like when she first asked him. Then perhaps, just maybe, Constance would still be alive. A lot of things might be different.

But no use dwelling on what could have been when there's still the future that needs to be taken care of.

"Did she say if others were working with her?" Robert asks.

"She said there was just Aiden, Captain Smythe, and Octavian," my father says. "But we know that two of them had followers. It's possible there may be others out there that she has control of, but if there are, I'll find them."

Robert gives my hand a squeeze. There's one less thing for me to worry about, though I want to assist my father in putting our country back together, even if it means finding more people who agree with Mother.

"What does this mean for us?" Robert asks. "I assume the wedding is off?"

I'm grateful to him for asking what I couldn't, but my heart drops. We've been through too much to add not having the wedding, but I don't know how we could hold it at this point. Not with being in mourning for a mother who's going to prison.

"The wedding is still on," my father says.

"What?" I respond. "That can't be."

"It needs to be. Unless, of course, you two don't want to get married."

"We do," I say. "We really, really want to."

"And it's far past time for it to happen," Robert says.

"I think the next step is to talk to your mother and the human king and queen," Father tells him, "but if they still approve, I don't see why we can't have a wedding tomorrow." He gives me hope that this is really going to take place.

Chapter
THIRTY-EIGHT

I TWIRL MY HAND in the skirt of my dress. No matter that Mother abhors the habit. Nothing she thought matters. I have to go off what I think is best.

"Don't worry," Robert says, taking my hand. "Everything is going to be fine. My mom already loves you, as do the king and queen."

"But what if they change their minds after they hear what my mother has done?"

"I won't let them." His words are reassuring. "Are you ready?"

"As ready as I'll ever be."

We walk in together. The human king and queen sit next to each other, Teresa and Dale on some chairs a little apart from theirs. The only other person in the room is Princess Belle. I feel bad being in here with them, for the pain Mother has caused them all. But they are familiar. The short time we spent together makes them less scary than they otherwise might be.

"What is it you two wanted to see us about?" the human king asks.

Robert tells them the entire story of what my mother did—the people she hurt, the rumors she started, and her motives for doing it all. He ends with saying how she's now going to prison for her crimes.

"As she well should," the queen says. "That woman has a lot of problems and shouldn't be left to rule a country. She cost me a son." She pulls out a handkerchief and dabs at her eyes.

I try not to let my nerves get the better of me. The idea hurts, but I try to hold my head high, like my mother taught me. She may have been wrong about a lot of things, but she was right about a few. "What we want to know is how you feel about us getting married tomorrow," I say.

The king and queen look at each other like they're having a whole conversation in that one glance. I wonder if Robert and I will ever be like that. Because no matter what they say, we'll still be getting married, one way or the other.

Teresa taps one finger against her lip, her eyes calculating. Dale looks at the floor. The longer the wait goes on, the less anticipation I have all will be well. It shouldn't be so hard to decide, should it? But maybe they don't want to be connected with a girl whose mother has done such horrible things—including the reason their son is dead.

"Of course they should still get married," Princess Belle says. "That's what Abner would have wanted and what's best for our people."

Hope fills me for the first time since we entered the room. Someone is on our side.

"I suppose he would have," the queen says.

Teresa looks deeply into her son's eyes. "I think this is what would be best."

"And it really would be good for the people to see our two countries unite. I hate what they'd think if we postponed it again," the king adds.

"We're getting married," Robert shouts. He grabs me in a hug and swings me around. "Tomorrow's the day."

Chapter
THIRTY-NINE

⌒

THE NIGHT BEFORE our wedding is one full of happiness, if not without a little tension and sorrow. I think of my mother as Robert and I lounge on a couch, Jocelyn doing handwork in a nearby corner. Mother is gone, but surprisingly, my father still insisted on us needing a chaperone. I guess we won't have need of one for much longer.

The room is silent. It has been ever since we came in here. There's a lot to think about.

"It's troublesome to believe my mother turned against us like that," I say.

"I can't believe it either," Robert says.

"I know she wasn't perfect—not by any means—but I thought she cared about the people instead of her selfish desires."

"It must have been difficult for her. It seems to me she thought she wasn't being selfish. That she was doing what was right for you."

"But all that time, everything from being sent into hiding on Sulamay Island to being kidnapped at my own wedding, to having Captain Smythe come after you seeking your life... All of it. She thought *that* was what was best for me? Best for the country? It's difficult to fathom."

"I won't disagree with you there. It's hard to understand what she was thinking," he says. "And now we need to figure out how to bring our countries together after they've been torn apart by one of their leaders."

"Our wedding will be a good first step," I say. "But do you think we can do anything about the stone the scroll talked about? Should we try to find it?"

"I don't know. I want our people to become the one they used to be, but I don't know how to start looking for that stone. We have so little to go on and no hints as to where else we might find it. It's too bad humans and elves need something like that to keep us together."

"Yeah," I say. But then, another thought hits me—something a lot more important than a simple stone. Really, what is a stone anyway, besides a jewel? "What if they don't need it? What if that was a way to keep our races feeling like they have something in common? I mean, mother started so many rumors and antagonized others, but what if she hadn't? Maybe our races would be closer than they are now."

He's silent a moment. "You have a point. And they've been working together well, fixing up the castle for our wedding."

"Plus there was that elf who saved your life."

"And Abner saved yours. If his opinion could change, anyone's can."

"So maybe we don't need some mythical thing to bring our people together?"

"I don't think we do."

What a perfect thought. Why didn't we think of it sooner? If magic is fading out in the world anyway, what's the point of trying to search for something magical? Something we have no ties to and no clues as to where it could be?

"I'm looking forward to working to uniting our people," I say.

"As am I."

"And we get to do this together."

Robert wraps an arm around my shoulders and pulls me closer to him on the sofa. "Together."

"After tomorrow, nothing will be left to stop us."

Chapter

FORTY

TODAY IS THE DAY. In just half an hour, I'll be a married woman. Nothing could be better. Well, unless Constance was here and my mother wasn't crazy.

So things aren't perfect. But they're still good.

"You look magnificent," Jocelyn says.

"Thank you. I like this dress a lot better than my last one." It's a sleek white silk, very simple, but elegant. I have on the necklace that I bought from the human merchants while we were traveling on Bardus.

"Robert will think you're the best looking thing he has ever seen," she says.

"That's a nice thought, but my opinion on it all has changed. It doesn't matter what anyone thinks—not mother, not Robert, not a single soul besides me. I am beautiful. I am worthwhile. I am strong."

Jocelyn grins. "That's the best thing I've heard all year."

"Now why don't you find something like that to think about yourself?"

She laughs. "I'm happy. For now, that's all that matters."

I hesitate before saying, "I know you loved Abner. Does it still hurt to have him gone?"

"Yes. Not as bad as it did, but I do miss him. We never would have worked out, anyway. I'm certain someday I'll find someone to be with."

"Only if I approve of him first," I tease.

"No one will dare try for my hand with you behind me with your sword and magic," she teases back. "Really though, I'm grateful I can count you as a friend."

"And I'm grateful you stuck with me long enough so we could become friends, and then stuck with me though being my friend meant hard things."

"I wouldn't have it any other way."

I smile, so happy to have a friend. Not just any friend, but her.

"It's time now," she says.

I try not to give a squeal of delight, but I'm so excited, it's difficult to hold it in. "This is it."

"It is. I'll lead you to your father, and then he'll take you down the aisle to Robert."

My father. He must be having such a difficult time with everything going on, yet here he is, supporting me. Just where I want him to be.

Father puts his arm out for me. I put a hand on it, and together, we walk. It's much different than we did it before, but I wanted to do things my way. A few steps forward, Robert's father awaits. He takes my other arm, and together, the three of us continue to where the people will be able to see us.

It was decided this would be the best way to define not only Robert and me uniting as husband and wife, but also both elf and human rulers. Especially after everything with my mother, we need a show of confidence.

We walk past the gauzy fabric that separates us from the crowd. There's a massive group of people on both sides of the aisle. With the help of workers and magic, the aisle is made of tiny flowers on beds of green. It's soft beneath my bare feet.

As we get closer, I only have eyes for the man at the end of the aisle. He's waiting there, just for me. Waiting to become my husband. Waiting for our first kiss.

It's the first time I get a look at Robert as he is for the wedding. He's wearing a simple suit in white to match my dress. Handsome, but not over done. Simple perfection.

My mouth tingles at the thought that I'll soon be pressing my lips to his. Soon, I'll be his wife.

My heart sings with joy. This is it. I'm getting married, and this time there's nothing to stop it. It goes by faster than I expected, faces on either sides of the aisle blurring. There's nothing but Robert and me.

As I reach him, the human king lets go of me and hands me to Robert. Then my father, the elven king, releases me to him. The human king steps up in front of us to officiate the ceremony. Since we're more on elf territory, we decided it would be better to have him do it than an elf, like we did last time.

He begins speaking, his words smooth and voice deep. I don't care about the words said to make us one. I care more that we are becoming one. That we are finally making this happen.

Robert gazes back down into my eyes. This is the moment we've been waiting for. That two entire nations have been waiting for.

Love emanates from his eyes. The same love I feel.

"Robert, do you have words for Arabella?" the king asks.

Robert smiles, warming my heart. "I love you more than life itself. I promise to honor and cherish you and your people, as long as there is breath left in my body. My soul will be devoted to you and your people."

"Arabella, do you have any words for Robert?" the king asks.

The joy surging through me at this moment is like nothing I've ever felt before. "You are the one man I want to spend the rest of my life with. I love you in a way words can never express. There's nothing I look forward to more than spending the rest of my days taking care of you and your people."

"With these words, you two bind yourselves together. Nothing shall tear you asunder," the king says. "You may now kiss the bride."

With a passion that stuns me, I kiss Robert. Our lips move together in perfect rhythm. There are shouts of joy, but they don't stop me from enjoying my first kiss. My heart blossoms with adoration for him.

His lips are soft yet firm against mine. Nothing will come between us. We are together now. Forever. As the cheering grows louder, our kiss deepens.

His masculine scent fills the air around me. He consumes me. I reach up and wrap my arms around his neck. Run my fingers through his hair and pull him closer. He wraps his arms around me and strokes my back. A trill of pleasure goes through me. This is what I want. What I need. Robert with me, as my husband.

We slowly part, only for him to pull me back in for a second kiss. The moment is a perfect one. I've never felt such excitement and happiness before. When we pull away for the second time, he kisses my forehead.

We turn to face those gathered. They are our people. Elf and human. We will work to make them more unified than ever before. We will find peace and harmony.

Together, we can do anything. We have become one, man and wife. Nothing can come between us, no matter how hard others may try. We'll work closely to bring us and our countries together. The strife between us is gone.

We are one.

about the
AUTHOR

AMAZON BEST SELLING author Janeal Falor lives in Utah with her husband and three children. In her non-writing time she teaches her kids to make silly faces, cooks whatever strikes her fancy, and attempts to cultivate a garden even when half the things she plants die. When it's time for a break she can be found taking a scenic drive with her family, fencing, or drinking hot chocolate.

SIGN UP TO RECEIVE RELEASE NOTIFICATIONS AT:

www.janealfalor.com

books in the
ELVEN PRINCESS SERIES

Bound by Birthright
Bound to Endure
Bound by Love

OTHER BOOKS BY JANEAL FALOR

MINE SERIES
Mine to Tarnish (Mine Prequel)
You Are Mine (Mine #1)
Mine to Spell (Mine #2)
Mine to Fear (Mine #3)
Sacrifice of Mine (Mine #4)

DARKENING LIGHT
Ever Darkening (Darkening Light #1)
Savage Light (Darkening Light #2)

ACKNOWLEDGEMENTS

~

THE LAST THREE BOOKS have been such a journey. I'm both elated and saddened that they are over. I don't know how I ever would have accomplished them if it were for the help of some amazing people.

Marie Krepps, thank you for beta reading, letting me bounce ideas off you, and just generally being a cool person.

Sotia Lazu has been such an incredible editor. I can't imagine these books without her help. Thank you for not throwing your laptop off the balcony, for saving me from having Arabella choke Robert, and many other things I can't even list. You are a gem!

My most excellent proofreader, Yesenia Vargas. A huge thanks to you for cleaning up my words and making them shine. I know this book would be a lot messier with out you.

Thank you to my family, for being there for me and patient while I hack away at my books. It's such a process, but you're always there. Not only are you patient, but you cheer me on and let me bounce ideas off of you.

Thank you to Erik for being the most fantastic husband ever. You are my everything, and your willingness to not just support me in this endeavor, but encourage me means the world to me.

To Tai, Xandria, and Will you are the best kids a mom could ever want. I love how you tell everyone about me and brag that your mom is a writer. Makes my day ever single time.

My most marvelous sister, Karen C. Eddington. These three book exist because of you. If you hadn't cheered me on and continually told me how much you love the story, it would have languished in a drawer at the very first one. There's not enough thanks in the world to tell me how much I appreciate you, but I say it anyway. Thank you!

And dear reader, I'd be remiss if I didn't thank you. Your encouragement and enthusiasm helped to push me on when I no longer felt like writing. You made me feel like this was a worth while venture. Thank you for all your notes of kindness and joy. They mean ever so much to me. Thank you.

www.ingramcontent.com/pod-product-compliance
Lightning Source LLC
Chambersburg PA
CBHW060327260626
47160CB00007B/2701